SELF-HELP FOR STONERS

STUFF TO READ WHEN YOU'RE HIGH

ROBERT CHAZZ CHUTE

Self-Help For Stoners
Stuff to Read When You're High

By Robert Chazz Chute

Published by Ex Parte Press
Copyright 2011 Robert Chazz Chute
ISBN 978-0-9877807-5-1
Interior design by Jeff Bennington at
www.jeffbennington.com
Cover design by Kit Foster at
www.kitfosterdesign.com

TABLE OF CONTENTS

DEDICATION

Two people inspired me most for this book: director, master raconteur and emperor of SModcast Kevin Smith, and Joe Rogan, comedian and Uber Pot Whisperer. These guys are twelve kinds of cool. What do Smith and Rogan have in common? Their art inspires art. Their thought begets thought.

In November 2010, I saw Kevin Smith on stage. I blogged about what I learned that night. Mr. Smith read my post and tweeted a little encouragement. That was the right push at the right time.

I have a long history in the publishing industry and I was already thinking about writing ebooks. But that was the problem: Too much thinking and not enough doing. I've turned my life upside down to write full-time. I'm a doer now.

I saw Mr. Rogan on stage at Massey Hall in Toronto in June, 2011 and love his podcast, The Joe Rogan Experience. Watching him have so much fun made me want to play, too, so I started a podcast as a companion to this book (*Self-help for Stoners*, later retitled All That Chazz.)

Thank you, gentlemen. You're both just the right mix of creativity, kindness, compassion and "Get off your ass!" This book reaches for, and I hope touches, your encouraging, truth-telling spirit. The fun is found in exploring lies that tell the truth.

Finally, I must dedicate this book to the most patient people the world, the people closest to me. Without Janice there would be no books. Without Ciara and Connor there would be no point. These wee few are the locks that keep me on the happy side of the doors of the insane asylum. My love to you all, always.

INTRODUCTION

Some people don't like the cannabis emblem, but they get the meaning all wrong. It's not merely an image promoting a naturally occurring drug. It's a symbol of autonomy over one's own consciousness. It's about your freedom to express yourself and your art. When I see a guy wearing a goofy t-shirt with a plant on it, I don't jump to the conclusion that he's a loser stoner; not all drinkers are alcoholics, either. What I see is someone with whom I share a common value: Each individual should have the right to be left alone if they aren't hurting anyone else. The emblem is about freedom, just as a book is a symbol of free thought.

Which brings us to Self-help for Stoners. A few good stories, parables, explorations and exhortations can fill an empty afternoon. A great story can fill your brain and transport you far away from banality. From the campfire circle after the hunt, to surfing the Internet with a cappuccino in hand, we escape into stories. Effective fiction and thought experiments possess ample power to juggle your brain chemistry. Self-help for Stoners can amp your dopamine and trigger neurotransmitter somersaults.

If you're hooked on reading and jonesing for some sugar, I'm glad you found this book. I've been waiting to sit you down to inject some happy into your head. There are bits where I'll ask you to join me in confronting our inner demons, too. Do so with compassion for yourself and please receive the message in the spirit it is sent: one ingredient of this book's self-help recipe. Squared away? Now we can begin our trip.

This book is about fun and escape, thought and surprise. I'm telling you up front that these stories will surprise you.

Then I'm going to surprise you anyway. Fiction is a magic trick plus a brain tickle that way, isn't it?

You don't have to be a stoner to enjoy this escape from reality. In fact, if you've ever watched South Park and The Daily Show with Jon Stewart, you've probably already exposed yourself to all the fun, all the moral lessons and thought experiments you'll ever need. But lessons are repeated until they are learned. (I know, because I've messed up, too.) We all crave art's high to make life more tolerable. We are all running from the reaper and that pitiless wraith will run us down and enfold us all, one by one. Fiction is a happy rest from that race.

In an article titled, Drugs and the Meaning of Life (www.samharris.org), author Sam Harris writes, "Everything we do is for the purpose of altering consciousness... Every waking moment — and even in our dreams — we struggle to direct the flow of sensation, emotion, and cognition toward states of consciousness that we value." Harris argues convincingly that in everything from the food we eat, the alcohol and caffeine we drink and the relationships we form, we're altering and diverting the mind flow.

We are comfort junkies and idea addicts and we're happily hooked on all kinds of highs. We are constantly trying to interpret our world and escape it, avoiding pain while pursuing pleasure. Add fiction to the list of things that alter your consciousness.

Please enjoy Self-help for Stoners with whatever stimulant you choose safely (because, as the costly failure of the War on Drugs has proved thoroughly, you'll do what you want to do, anyway.) I advocate fiction itself for your high. Stories are harmless, portable, easy to stick in your head, have zero dire side effects and they're legal just about everywhere.

This book is a magic mirror. It is only an illusion that it's full of stories about other people. Look closer. You will see yourself in others. You'll find yourself staring back from the page. Reading is ultimately an exercise in compassion, because there is no Us and Them. There is only Us.

Happy reading! Enjoy your trip.

~ Chazz

Legs Gabrielle
Breaks Out

As you roll into town, you find yourself babbling to Chili about the sights, such as they are. "There's where I went to elementary school. There's the bank. There's the high school football field. Under those bleachers is where I let my first boyfriend disappoint me horribly."

"I recognize that line," Chili says.

"Oh, look, there's the town post office...in case you forgot how to read signs on the flight down here."

"Thanks, boss. All small towns look alike to me, but maybe Poeticule Bay seems a little familiar because of your act."

"This is the epicenter of what was, Chill. The nadir before the zenith, the shit before the flush."

"Whatever you say." Chili steers the Escalade into a parking spot. He's flummoxed when he sees no parking meter. "I grew up in Chicago and moved to L.A. as soon as I could. I've never been to a town so small."

"No parking meters and not one traffic light. It's super rural Maine. Think Amish but without the Amish flair for technological progress and fun on a Saturday night."

"Ba-dum-bump!"

"Yeah, yeah. My town is so small..."

"How small is it?"

"My home town is so small — " you begin.

"I know! I know! No bigger than my dick!"

This is old material but you both laugh. As your friend, bodyguard and general do-all, one of Chili's duties is to keep up morale. And you need that now. You need it hard, so you don't mind his phony chuckle at all.

Chili punches a button and unlocks your door. "You sure you don't want me to go in and pick up the flowers, boss?"

"Nope. I'm in no rush to get home. I can't show up without flowers or my sister won't start off with 'Hello, it's been ages.' She'll start off with, 'Where's the fucking flowers?' "

"Lovely," Chili says.

When you step out from behind the safety of the Escalade's tinted windows, people freeze. Something has changed. The few people on the street, young and old, all have cell phones. That's new. And they're all whipping them out to take pictures of you. Just like home.

You glance back through the open door and you can tell Chili's irritated. He's used to walking ahead of you, a massive muscled arm out front, ushering you through the world. You think, where were you when I was walking through the gauntlet of mean girls in high school? But that's old material, too, so it's time to let it go and keep that stuff between you and your therapist from now on.

The girl behind the counter goes stiff as you walk in. You smile and ask for a dozen yellow roses. She doesn't move. She stares, brain gears grinding.

"Yes," you say as gently as you can. "I'm her." You produce a fifty. "Tell everybody I pulled that bill out of my bra and you can probably sell it on eBay to some creepy whacko." That makes her laugh and has the added benefit of getting her skull engine in gear.

A crowd gathers outside in the time it takes the girl to get the roses from the fridge. The telephone tree must be working, alerting the villagers that the monster they made here has returned. You grab the roses, tell her to keep the change and breeze back into the truck without getting sucked into any smiles or allowing someone to grab your hand. The trick is to move with purpose, smile and keep moving. "Hi! Hi! Gotta go! Sorry! Bye!" Rinse, repeat. Ad infinitum.

"Legs! Legs!" someone implores from the sidewalk, but Chili already has the Escalade in gear.

You wonder if you managed to strike the right note of decorum since you're home for a funeral. Once, after a night on the red carpet, a couple of movie critics wrote, "Legs tries to make her smile look friendly, but her eyes just say, 'Nyah, nyah-ni-nyah, nyah!' "

Like always, Chili says the right thing at just the right time. "Home town girl makes good."

You give him a wry smile. You wish the voice in your head was so kind. "You know better than that. Just as often it's, 'I knew her in high school and she wasn't so funny.' Or, 'I thought she was taller.' Or 'Who does she think she is?' Turn left at the next stop sign, Chil."

"That's just words," Chili says as he turns the wheel. "A little mean, maybe, but better than all those dudes peeking in windows or climbing fences."

"I know. So many sperm donors, so little time. And not enough condoms, penicillin and flea collars in the world." You watch for his teeth in the rear-view mirror, but you do better than a smile. He throws his head back as he laughs and you know it's real. One of the things you love about Chili is his reactions have to be honest. He was a terrible actor before he was your bodyguard.

"On the right with the big oak tree in the front yard."

"The one that —?"

"I swore I'd hang myself from if I didn't get to go to prom, yeah."

When you spot The Little Beige House of Parental Tyranny, the anxiety rises. Out of reflex, you look for some gratification from your audience of one. "The courts should have a dedicated hotline to expedite paperwork for celebrities hounded by stalkers. Like...1-800-RESTRAINING ORDER."

Chili laughs politely.

"A swing and a miss, huh?"

Chili shrugs. "The troubles of the overly privileged probably won't play well in the red states."

"Maybe if I do the East Indian call center voice and amp it up."

"Sounds hideous."

"Hey, hey! Girl with dead father here! Girl with dead father who signs your exorbitant checks!"

"Sounds great, boss."

"Nah, you were right the first time." Before you reach for the passenger door, you reach over the seat and squeeze his shoulder.

Then photographers emerge, two from parked cars across the street and two from behind a hedge.

"I stay away from this town since I was eighteen years old and this is the thanks I get." You wanted to put more breeze and bounce in your delivery, but instead you sound like you discovered a dead squirrel at the bottom of your shampoo bottle.

"Go straight inside," Chili says. "I'll do my big and black thing."

"Careful. They're rural. They'll be more than suitably terrified. You might kill them with a hard look."

"Only if you want me to, boss."

Walking into the house should have worked fine but the front door is locked. The cameras click away behind you as you stand on the porch ringing and ringing the doorbell. When Jacqui finally lets you in, your cheeks are burning. The headline will read: Legs Gabrielle, Not Welcome.

"Hey," Jacqui says.

You hug her. It's like putting your arms around a fire hydrant in January. "Hi, sis. I tried to call on the way from the airport."

"The phone keeps ringing. I finally took it off the hook."

Jesus, you think. *Incommunicado? Really? I either come from an alien culture or I left to live among aliens.* "Keep the door open a hair," you say. "Chili will be here in a minute."

"You brought people? I really don't think that's appropriate. Couldn't you have left your entourage —?"

"Chili is a big guy, but he's only one guy. You start calling him my 'entourage' and he's going to start feeling self-conscious about his weight."

"Ha," Jacqui says. "Ha." Bloodless.

"So we're already fighting?" you say. "Is that the plan? I just came for a funeral. I left my boxing gloves and slingshots in my party clutch purse."

Chili fills the doorway and gives your little sister his sweetest smile. To her shock, he gives her a kiss on both cheeks before he says anything at all. Damn him, you can tell he's genuine. That's not Hollywood horseshit. The bastard is sweet and means it.

When he sees your jaw hanging open, he guesses, correctly, that it's up to him for the formal introduction. "Chili Gillie," he says. His high voice always takes newcomers off guard. He has the look, but that high voice of his didn't get him past a first audition unless it was a seriously bad no-budget comedy. "Your sister calls me her handsome, hairless assistant, but I'm just here to help out. You need anything, you let Chili know."

Jacqui nods and you can almost see her knees turning to warm wax. Chili has this effect on both women and men. He's effortlessly charming. Sometimes he makes you wish you were a gay guy, too, but Chili's so smooth, he'd cheat on you within a week.

"The funeral is at three. I didn't think you'd get here in time," Jacqui says. "It wouldn't have looked good for your fans if you missed your own father's service."

The way she hits the word "fans" makes clear she thinks people who like your brand of humor are idiots and she's no idiot. They way she said "your own father" makes your upper lip curl, too. She must be a bitch on wheels with those luckless third graders she teaches.

"I'm very sorry for your loss," Chili tells Jacqui.

Again, you look at Chili in awe. It would never have occurred to you to answer your sister's passive aggression with kind words. The family pattern has always been: when somebody sticks a knife in your back, pull it out and have a knife fight.

You sit in the den, the room that, on stage and in high school, you often called "Dad's Petty Fiefdom of Horrors." You look around the room. It looks the same. "When you last saw him, did Dad say anything?"

Jacqui sits behind Dad's desk, like this is a job interview. "The last I saw Dad, all he said was that we were out of bread and that I should bring home a loaf after work. Those were his last words," Jacqui says.

You look at the pictures on the mantel: Dad in his navy uniform; Mom just before she died; Jacqui in a cap and gown, holding her diploma. There are thousands, maybe hundreds of thousands of pictures of you out in the world. Not one has somehow squeezed into this room.

"Maybe those weren't his last words," you say. "Maybe he got a call from a telemarketer and got to tell somebody off one more time before his stroke. That would be nice for him."

Jacqui looks sour.

"We can hope," you shrug.

"Sheila!"

Before you two can start bickering, Chili picks up the picture of your father in his dress whites. "He was a handsome man. Will there be a picture like this at the service? It's a good picture. Or...will there be a viewing?"

"Viewing? Oh. No. My father's already been cremated."

My father, you note. Not our father. Well, maybe that's kind of appropriate. When this was your childhood home, it certainly wasn't "Our father who art in heaven." It was "Our father who art always pissed because what the baby of the family thinks is funny is really too much back-sass."

When you come back from the Land of Lost in Thought, you can tell Chili has been busy melting your sister's knees again. His charm is a blowtorch as long as he doesn't have to fake it for a movie audition.

Jacqui makes him tea in the kitchen. You hear her say, "How does one get a name like Chili?"

"One gets it because Gillie was the name I was born with. I got saddled with William at birth. Now, William's a nice name. But Willy Gillie? Ridiculous."

"Did you choose Chili because of that character John Travolta played in that movie?"

"Used to tend bar in a Mexican restaurant," he says.

She giggles, which you can't remember her ever doing. Chili is your No Man's Land between what you were and what everybody thinks you are now.

The house smells the same. It's not a bad smell. It's just that every home's smell is a distinct mixture of the people who live there. There's a bit in there somewhere and you dig out your notebook. Something like, "Every house smells different. My childhood home smells like a blend of daffodils, fear and the sweat of racists." After another moment's thought, you scratch out "blend" and pencil in "dour cornucopia".

But you remind yourself you're trying to move away from that kind of material. Go back to the same well too many times and you go from bitter-funny to shtick-funny to maligned hack. You take more notes: If I keep my game up, I'll be a has-been faster than I can say, "Remember me? I thought it would last forever but fame went so quickly I'm now considering taking up an addiction so I can get on a shitty reality show. I've never done meth but I'm willing to learn. Please love me." Shaky start and too long around the bases for a home run...but that "Please love me"? That has potential for a bit.

As worried as you are about repeating the small-town American mind material, the hardcore fans love that stuff. The fans want more of the same. Everyone is in love with preconceptions, so a little small-town mindset lives in everybody. Your agent, Mort, wants you to make your onstage persona sweeter to show you're growing and changing "into a range".

"Persona? What persona?" you asked Mort, genuinely mystified. "That's me on stage, you asshole. If I could pretend childhood pain this easy, I'd have three Oscars already."

Mort wants you to move from the quirky pretty girl to the lead in a couple of rom-coms next year. He has you seeing a nutritionist to make you angry and anorexic; working out with a personal trainer to make you so buff women will hate you; and talking with a therapist to transform you from a bitter, hilarious stand-up comic into a much less funny, neurotic actress who men will find "sexy instead of scary." That could work. Or maybe you should fire Mort's ass and torch his Porsche.

When you look up from your notebook, Chili pokes his head into the den and his face says, "Help me!" Before you can say anything, he excuses himself to field phone calls. The bastard's running away. You had to wait years before you could run away.

Jacqui comes back into the den. She carries her teacup to Dad's desk. "Are you and Chili...?" she says coolly.

"Constantly. He exhausts me. But when you pay for it, man-whores have to deliver every time."

"Uh-huh."

What is it about coming home that makes you rabid about riffing? You can't seem to help yourself. So you resolve to play nice. You take a deep breath. "Jacqui, I have a secret to share with you."

"Oh?"

"The last weekend before I left home was Labor Day weekend. You and Dad went up to the cabin and I had this great idea. I promised myself I was going to make it to Hollywood and make it big. I wanted to commemorate the beginning of my career, so I found a case in the attic and I made a time capsule. I buried it — "

"In the corner of the garden. I know," Jacqui says.

You have one of those rare moments when your brain empties out so fast, the wind makes a whooshing sound and you have no idea what to say. The inside of your skull feels like it's lined with peppermint gum.

"You didn't bury it very deep. It came up a little. The frost heaved it up three years ago. Dad was upset. He looked for that aluminum case for a long time before he spotted it planting beans. He was sure you had stolen it before you took off, which, I guess you did."

"I was eighteen," you say.

"So?"

"Dad took you to the lake and left me to my own devices. It-it seemed like a grand gesture before the big expedition."

"I was only nineteen," Jacqui says, "but I would never have done that."

And the silence stretches out. Your sister, it occurs to you, was born middle-aged. Risking nothing, she had never made any mistakes. That tragic level of success had made Jacqui unbearably smug. She didn't have any funny stories, like the one about the manager who sent you to a porn audition. Or how you got a new manager and you had to fire her for doing the same thing.

"I have stuff in the time capsule I want," you say.

"I know," Jacqui says. She sips her tea, pinky out.

"Did you go through it?"

"The songs? And the jokes? Yeah. I can see why you want them back."

You take a few more deep breaths. Chili is still in the backyard, off the battlefield. "The case. Where is it?"

"Yeah, about that," Jacqui says. "Dad was angry."

"Royally pissed, you mean. As I recall, he had no other emotional settings." (And critics say you don't have range.)

"Royally pee-o'd, yes," Jacqui says primly. "He never got over you taking the tuition money to run off to California. Hollyweird, he called it."

"My gamble worked out, don't you think?"

"Yes. You were very lucky, Sheila. Dad called you Lottery Girl."

You sigh. "Earlier you asked how Chili got his name. Did you ever wonder how I got mine?" Before she can answer, you add, "If you use the word 'spreading', I'll make you eat that teacup and you'll choke on the saucer."

She shrugs. She puts the teacup down and to the side of the desk, away from you.

"Did you watch my first HBO special?"

"I saw it on DVD eventually," Jacqui says. "Dad couldn't get through the first half when it was on TV. You went off to your glamorous life and made a mint tearing down your hometown, burning down your family. We had to stay here, Sheila. You embarrassed us. Dad and I lost friends."

"I guess you couldn't make very good friends, then. I would have thought Dad would be more worried about losing a daughter." You take another breath. You feel hot, like the air is going out of the room. "Mom would have laughed her ass off at my act. You were always Daddy's little girl and I was Mom, but shorter. I wish she were here now."

Chili comes in, too late. "You want me to dig that thing out of the garden, boss?"

"Apparently I didn't bury the body deep enough, Chili. Dad dug it up already."

"You should have seen it, Chili," Jacqui says. "All that teen angst stuffed into one case smelled pretty sour."

"Hm," Chili says.

"Jacqui was just wondering how I got my show biz name, Chili."

"Not desperately," your sister says.

Chili smiles. "Few think to ask. I mean, look at her." He gestures your way. "They see your sister's gams and think her nickname is too obvious."

"I wanted to be called Gams Gabrielle," you say, "but the only focus group that liked that was from the 1920s, so Legs it was."

Chili ignores you and pushes on. "Management never disabused anyone of the sexy assumption. In fact, for every tour and press jacket and movie, they put her in shorter and shorter skirts. Driving home the Legs Gabrielle brand, you know?"

Chili opens his custom double-breasted suit and squats to perch his bulk on the ottoman. The room looks like it has shrunk around him. "But the truth is different," he continues. "The boss went on her first audition. She comes in cracking jokes. Your sister's got more charisma in her little toe than most actors put out there in a year with a staff of five writers to make them look clever. On camera or on stage, your sister doesn't know nervous."

Jacqui looks at you, but she still sees the brat who ran off to Hollyweird. Dad's been drilling that image into her head for eight years.

"The boss goes through the audition and everybody's breathless. She flipped the table around. You know what that means?"

Jacqui shakes her head, but her face says she doesn't care.

"To flip the table around in an audition means that the person auditioning isn't getting judged. Instead, the boss was in the position of deciding whether the movie is good enough for her to bother. First audition and she stands out that far. Everybody knows instantly that your sister is going to be huge. They expect pretty, but they never expect pretty to be married up with that smart and really funny."

Chili can see that Jacqui isn't impressed, but he presses on. "Sheila became Legs Gabrielle that afternoon. The director turned to the producer and said, 'Triple threat.'" Chili looks at you with shining eyes. You wish your father could have faked that look just once. "The director says, 'Sheila, your career is going to have legs. We just have to change your name and you're a shining golden goddess.'"

"Lipshitz was great for stand-up..." you say.

"Lipshitz is a burden," Jacqui says. "But Legs Gabrielle made it worse."

"Thanks for telling her, Chili. If I'd told it, she might have thought I was bullshitting. Around here it seems I have another name: Lottery girl."

A cloud crosses Chili's face. "But lottery implies luck, not talent."

"Oh, you've done very well for yourself," Jacqui admits.

But why add "for yourself"? Does that imply you should have brought her out west so her sneering could have point-blank impact?

"So can I have my stuff?" you ask.

Jacqui shifts in her seat and, before she can say anything, you've guessed. "Dad destroyed everything in my time capsule, didn't he?"

Jacqui breaks into a huge smile. "Dad was more creative than you ever gave him credit for. You didn't get it all from Mom."

Chili is already getting up and buttoning up.

"Dad got cremated. You'll be able to visit his ashes, along with the ashes of your little time capsule, at the family plot. I suppose if you want to retrieve your hateful little jokes and song lyrics, you could sift through them at the cemetery. Bring a shovel to dig up the urn. The photographers would sure enjoy that."

You're so stunned you don't move. Chili's standing beside you, hand out, pleading with his eyes to get the hell out of here.

"You should also know, Sheila, that Dad was so pissed, you aren't in the will at all. You might have been had you called more often."

You clear your throat and stand to tower over her. "I asked you to get Dad to come to my show when I was on tour many times. He could never tear himself away from his garden. Or did he even get half of my messages?"

Jacqui goes white and says quietly, "Am I to expect you to get a bunch of high-priced lawyers to fight Dad's bequest to me?"

You consider that for just a moment and then shake your head. "Honey, I'm going to get much more material out of the half hour I've been here. Financially speaking? I will make a metric fuck ton of cash off you forever. Emotionally? Eviscerating you over and over on stage will be worth much more money than anything Dad could leave me. You just bought me another mansion in the Hollywood Hills, bitch."

At the door you turn back and take the framed picture of your mother. Jacqui looks like she might run at you for it, but changes her mind when you hand it to Chili. "I'll just take this with me," you say. That's all I need now. From Mom I got my sense of humor. From you and Dad, all I ever got was all the emotional pain that fuels my success."

Hands balled into fists, Jacqui screams, "Don't bother calling if you ever need a kidney!"

You smile. "That's funny, Jacqui. There might be hope for you yet. Of course, if I ever need a kidney, I'll just have you killed."

You're out the door, steaming for the Escalade. Chili rushes ahead and opens the door for you. He keeps the photographers back, but they jump to shoot around him.

The headlines will read: Too verklempt to attend her father's funeral. But the real fans will forgive you that. Tears of anguish stream down your face. This will be good for your brand.

People call it Hollyweird, but it's no stranger than any small town in America. If you look closely, celebrities are very much like actual human beings.

Mind Bend

A voice, dark and foreboding, tells you you're getting paranoid. It says the cops are outside, that you're being watched, that the walls hide judging eyes. That voice? It's your voice.

Through a bar of light in the Venetian blinds? No cops. All you see is a feathery tentacled fog floating over glistening grass. You wish you could hide in dew's morning stars. Instead, the great white blanket coils around the world, tightening around your house, pressing the walls in, a closing noose.

People say you're addicted to drugs. They don't get it. You're addicted to the change in your perception. Hallucinations? No. These are enhancements, expanding your awareness of the shrinking space between things. You don't see a chair, a table, a sofa, a TV. You see the space among them and it almost seems to mean something important. Almost.

Rockets will never take you to black holes in the center of each galaxy's glazed donut, but you can see between the stars and into the infinite dark from here. You can feel the smooth weight of the moon if you reach out with your mind.

Just close your eyes.

The Foreseeable

When the boss introduces you to his hot daughter and you shake her hand, keep your eyes on hers and smile, but not so big. Just flick your eyes down at that amazing rack some other time. Do not stare at the rack.

But you've already lost. Why is it so hard not to do something when you know it's a stupid thing to do?

When the boss says his daughter will be a summer intern, just nod and say something neutral. "We sure have a lot of work to do around here, so some help will be great." That would have been good.

Resist the urge to suck in your gut when she floats through your office. Keep your eyes on your computer screen. Do not slide that picture of your wife and kid into your desk drawer. Do not, under any circumstances, get caught looking at her ass as she bends over to put files in the bottom drawer.

When the boss's daughter sends you a sext message in the middle of your Power point presentation, erase it. Do not keep the evidence in your Blackberry for later reading. Do not look at her again until you're saying, "Goodbye and good luck with your second year at college." Pray she meets a nice boy who lives in Wisconsin and she never interns at her daddy's company again.

When she says, all cool and smirky, that you looked kind of flustered during your presentation, tell her, "No, I'm fine, thank you." As if you're an anatomically incorrect robot, say, "I think you sent a text message to me in error. It must have been meant for your boyfriend so I deleted it without really reading it."

Do not look in her eyes too long and say, "I guess I was distracted." (That was a mistake.) By all that's holy, do not smile and say, "And you know why. Don't pretend you don't. You're too mature a young woman to pretend."

Pretend you're a mature man and do not lose your job over this. You know where this is going. Shut it down before it's too late.

When she amped up the flirtation and sent you a picture of herself in a bikini? That would have been a good time to assert yourself. Tell her you're flattered, but you're not interested. Then add, "Gotta go! I really need to get home to my pregnant wife."

When she persists and sends a shot of her in a bikini without the bikini top? You could have saved your job right there if you'd told her you're really gay and she's too hippy for you anyway. Recommending Jenny Craig to her in a thoughtful, concerned tone would definitely have saved your marriage.

When the rest of the staff left the office by five-thirty and she said, with that lascivious smile, that she planned to work late? That would have been a good time to fake a call from your wife. If you had grabbed your coat and run out screaming that your wife was having contractions three months before her due date? That would have been a good play and you'd be holding your baby now.

When the girl kissed you, you shouldn't have kissed her back, of course. No tongues would have been a smarter move. Reaching up to feel the weight of her breasts under that thin, white blouse? Well, let's not kid ourselves. By then you weren't making choices. By the time she knelt in front of you, your brain was not operating with the usual required blood flow.

But there were choices that could have been better: Not doing it on the boss's desk, for instance; locking the door; making sure the boss himself wasn't squirreled away in the conference room with a client; wearing a condom.

Instead, when your boss walked into his office, there you were in the throes of ecstasy, banging the boss's daughter doggy style on his desk yelling, "Ride it, bitch! Ride it!"

There's no established etiquette for that. Say you're sorry, of course, but since you're about to get thrown into a shit storm no matter what you do, you might as well come, right? It's not like you can get into more trouble, right? You're just as damned either way, so when you look up as that door swings open, the ejaculate is both squeezed and scared out of you.

Remember that moment as if it's your last. (Your company does sell guns, after all, and the boss has a legendary temper.)

As often as this has happened in the world — and you know it's happened a lot — no one knows what to do next in this scenario. Do you grab your clothes and put on your pants, hopping around yelling your apologies? Or do you just run naked into the parking lot and hope you left your company car unlocked?

Do not say, "She started it." That's for sure.

When you are on the ground and her father, your ex-boss, is kicking you in the balls repeatedly with his shiny size thirteen shoes? Don't beg him for mercy. Instead beg the pie plate-eyed client standing there uselessly with his jaw hanging open.

Plead with him to call the police. This will have terrible ramifications later, but in the short term, it may save one of your testicles, anyway.

When you are handcuffed to a hospital bed, do not ask the doctor to take a picture of your penis. That bright red ring of lipstick is not evidence against the boss's daughter that will be useful in court.

When the police officer informs you that the summer intern is not returning to her second year of college this fall, make sure to look as confused as possible. When the police officer informs you that the young woman will be returning to classes in the fall but the classes are in grade ten? Piss yourself and induce vomiting if it doesn't occur spontaneously.

Don't ask for your job back while you're waiting for your trial. Don't ask to hold on to the company car for another week. Don't call the company to ask for your last check. Don't complain when the company health plan refuses to cover your medical bills as a workplace injury. And no, they won't pay for your legal assistance, either. There is only legal punishment.

Don't even ask another employee — somebody you considered a buddy— to gather your personal belongings from your desk. The court order says no contact and that means no contact. Besides, all your shit was thrown into the bonfire (atop the boss's desk) in the back lot. The boss burned it all up and threw a half-empty bottle of vodka on top to make sure it burned bright.

Do not look shocked when you wobble out of the cab from jail (still in your hospital gown) to find all your clothes on the front lawn. It's been raining all weekend so all your possessions have been soaking in mud for three days.

That's what was happening to your stuff as you sat in a holding cell enduring the jeers from a vagrant boozehound who alternately howls at the guards and mumbles that he wants to hear you tell the story again and again as he masturbates with grim determination.

When you show up on your college buddy's doorstep — your oldest friend — do not ask his pregnant wife (and your wife's best friend) to "be reasonable." When the college buddy says, "Cheryl doesn't want you staying on our couch," take the hint. Don't say, "It's just for a few nights." It's not just for a few nights.

Your college buddy was good for a few rounds of pool and a bullshit session once in a while. He is useless for apocalyptic events. Just ask him for some money for a motel and thank him because this is the last time you'll ever see him.

When the judge sends you off to prison for a short stay, resign yourself to the knowledge that this will not feel like a short stay. When your cellmate, who has more tattoos than teeth, hurts your feelings with unnecessarily caustic remarks, do not lose your temper. When you lose that fight and he bends you over a chair and orders you to spread your cheeks? Take it like a man and ride it, bitch! Ride it!

When you get out and try to make up with your wife, don't expect much. It will not serve you to explain that you picked up herpes in prison, not from the girl. Just be happy the court allows you to spend a little time with your baby, though the visits will be supervised until your baby is eighteen years old.

When the boss's daughter shows up at your bachelor apartment, don't even go near the door. When you fail to hide under your narrow bed, just yell through the door that she's already destroyed you. You have nothing left for her to take.

When you open the door a crack, it's too late. You are lost again.

Don't let your eyes linger over the broken orbit of her swollen left eye, the fresh black and blue rising, the old yellow bruises slowly evaporating last. Under no circumstances should you look at the baby in her arms. You should not examine the dark curly hair, just like yours.

You're in no condition to help anyone. You can't even help yourself, stupid.

She says it's yours, but she's lied before.

But anyone with a fat wallet can help someone. Maybe the impossibility of the task is what makes it noble. For the same reason you fought all that good advice, maybe you should try the impossible. The forbidden pulls like a black hole's gravity. The quixotic is exotic.

Redemption is unattainable. So what? Allowing others to define you by one mistake, or even a series of mistakes? That's wallowing.

Your only hope is to begin again.

Same Thing
Only Different

Why do so many stoners talk about the potential of a time machine? They're already high. Life's not going to get better. Sure, sure. Go back and kill Hitler. We're all agreed. (Yawn) Then what, Captain Time Travel? You go back and have that threesome you were too chickenshit to follow through on the first time?

That's just Round One.

Now that you've erased one timeline's regrets, you will replace them with fresh mistakes. One of those sluts from the threesome gave you herpes while the other fell in love with you. The one who loves you rats you out to your girlfriend and ruins your life.

Next thing you know, you're firing up your time machine again.

New timeline, Round Two, will be every kind of suck but the warm, happy kind. This time you're living in a trailer park with ugly kids and a herpes-ridden wife who's addicted to crack and rage.

So you whip out your handy-dandy time machine for Round Three. The worlds change, but one common denominator is constant, despite all the variables revolving around you. You're still dragging the same shitty you making new batches of rancid mistakes. You never see the new mistakes coming.

Round after round, you zip back in time trying to fix things. You've got a mansion and everything's cool until you back over your three-year-old in the driveway. You win the lottery again and again, but every time, in every new dimension, everybody still hates your fat, rich guts. Never mind zipping around with the time machine you'll never have. The one fate you can never escape is you.

Instead, peer through the magic smoke to your future. Your mind is a time machine. Work those dials. You can see your future from the couch. You're the same, only swollen. That ugly plaid couch just gets rattier and rattier. The future is no mystery. It's the present stretched out.

To change the future, change your present. Get up from the couch. Aspire, do it and inspire. Stop planning. Go! Go before the future punches you in the dick and bitch slaps you with the herpes-infected fist of The Truth About You.

Another Day at the Office

As soon as you see those flashing red, blue and white lights strobing in your rear view mirror, you begin to sweat and you rehearse saying in a calm voice, "Is there a problem, officer?"

Of course there's a problem. A cop has just pulled you over. That's only good if the kidnapper with the sawn off is driving and you're the one duct taped in the trunk. But that scenario hardly ever comes up.

The officer sidles up. What is with these guys? Why do they all have that same moustache and sunglasses? Do they get a bulk discount? Is it a policy that says they all have to look alike or does that happen on its own? And they all have that walk, holding the belt and coming up slow, like he has spurs on his boots going *ka-ching, ka-ching, ka-ching*. Like he's got six guns on each hip and he's primed to slap leather.

This cop has swagger, but he's a careful one. The cop chews gum and peers in the back window first. When he sees the big box in the back seat he slows down another half step just to process what he's seeing.

He stops and leans one hand on the trunk to make sure the latch is caught so your best and craziest buddy won't pop out of that big trunk and cut him in two with .00 load from an altered pump shotgun with five shots.

Shrewd cop. He doesn't hurry. He's thinking what you're about. Civvies call it a traffic stop, but cops call it a takedown, with all the ominous connotations the word implies.

You have the license and registration out and ready. Your eyes are watering but you look back with your best disarming smile. Your other hand is on the wooden dowel under the blanket. The dowel reaches into the cage in the backseat.

You tap the window button and as soon as it comes down an inch the cop steps back. Before he can order you to put both hands on the wheel, you jiggle the stick. There's a hiss from the cage and wham! The noxious spray shoots out to fill the car. Again.

"Whew!" the cop yells and jumps back, plugging his nose.

You can't pretend watery eyes away, but your smile appears open and friendly and five kinds of dumb. "Was I driving too fast, officer? I have to pee real bad and I was hoping for an off ramp soon."

"Whew!" the cop says again and shakes his head hard, as if that will stop the stench from crawling up his nostrils and hammering his brain stem.

As bad as it is for him, it's ten times worse for you. But jail would be much worse, so you just grit your teeth and jiggle the dowel again. Can't let the stinking little beast get complacent.

"Is that what I think it is?" the cop says, already knowing the answer but unable to construct a scenario where this makes sense.

"Skunk! Yessir! I'm taking him to get them ass glands taken out."

"What? Why?" The cop has totally forgotten to ask for the license and registration in your hand, which is good because that paperwork does not belong to you.

"Skunks make great pets," you say. "You get them ass glands taken out and it's just like a purty black and white kitten. See, we live out in the woods. My daddy used to get rid of skunks when they crawled under the porch. He got rid of 'em with a twelve gauge, you know? But that's kinda cruel. You pour a little ammonia around your front step and them'll stay away just fine. Keeps raccoons out of the garbage, too, if that's your problem."

The officer has taken another step back so you're leaning out the window now, shouting back, eager and cooperative as traffic roars past.

"So, my little girl? She's six and cute as a bug's butt? She says, 'Daddy, can I have the skunk under the porch? He's cute, just like Pepe Lepew.' The wife didn't like that idea at all. You know how that goes. But who can look into the eyes of a six-year-old and say no, am I right?"

The thing in the cage hisses and you wish this cop would make up his mind because you are about to throw up. Again.

"So I've gotta piss like the proverbial race horse and a few exits back I tried to get into a restroom but the gas station prick wouldn't let me have the key so I could relieve myself. Can you beat that? Wouldn't allow a man a little dignity. I might be stinky, but I got a butt load of human kindness in me."

The cop laughs and backpedals. He's not going to touch the license and registration in your hand. He won't ask any more questions. He won't look in the trunk. He certainly won't haul you out and put you in the back of his cruiser.

"I just got a couple of more exits and I'll get to the vet who will do the job, 'kay?"

"Yeah! Go! Go!" He waves you on. Nice fella.

For all your suffering, you gave him a fair exchange. He'll tell this story for the rest of his life. And you'll avoid the overly punitive pot laws in the otherwise great state of Texas. You'll also avoid the consequences of some more universally accepted laws, come to think of it.

You peel away, gravel flying, and roll down the windows. It doesn't help a bit.

You got the idea for this dodge when a buddy called your latest crop "skunk weed." That was right before he kidnapped you at gunpoint and forced you to take him to your secret stash in the woods. He followed the map fine, but the ruts in the logging roads were so deep you banged your head on the underside of the trunk lid until you thought your brains would shit out of your ears.

Bang. Bang. Bang.

Your ears were still ringing when you popped open that trunk and beat him down with the tire iron. Then you took his shotgun with .00 load.

Bang. Bang. Bang.

Which was overkill. Now you have a skunk in the back seat and the trunk is stuffed full of weed and bloody chunky buddy. On the way to Vegas, you can bury bloody buddy in the desert along with an irritated skunk, but there ain't enough skunkweed nor tomato juice baths in the world to make you smell right.

You should have been an accountant. If you were, you wouldn't always have to carry a knife in your sock. You wouldn't be afraid to tell a friend where you live. You could be banging a secretary on the boss's desk right about now, if you were a luckier guy.

The sad thing? If your bloody, chunky buddy in the trunk had just asked for some weed and a loan, you would have obliged with a smile. As you drive on, most of the water in your eyes is from skunk.

Face Off

Some days you feel so sick, the only answer is to jack off and, doing your best Jason Statham impression, you give yourself a tough guy pep talk in the mirror.

Some people look like they never have a down day. They skydive before breakfast and that's the slowest part of their day. They make money by speaking into a microphone or looking into a camera. A small army makes their visions happen. Fans follow them no matter what they do.

And you're still on the couch, still clueless what you're next move will be. You're still a consumer, not a maker, producer, seller. You produce belly button lint and carbon dioxide.

Occasionally you carry heavy things for low pay. You may never be Jason Statham or Kevin Smith or Lady Gaga or Brad Pitt or Johnny Depp or Joe Rogan or Stephen King or JK Rowling or Batman...okay, let's face it. You aren't going to be any one of those people.

But you could be the better you that you dream of. You could change. Or you could turn on the TV for just one more hour.

Choose.

How Irwin
Changed His Name

Your older brother was the only Irwin in the whole school. Mom named him (which proves she's petty and he was an accident, too.) He doesn't look like much, passed out, drooling, snoring and smelling of stale beer. No one can handle that much alcohol, so his body has gone to Plan B: sweat it out. But Irwin is a man and you still feel like a boy even though you're only a year younger. Your brother found a way to claim a new name and make it stick. This is how Irwin became Jack.

You never understood Man-language. Men claim friendship is everything — bros before hoes — but when you watch your brother with his boys, their exchanges are cruel, casual contempt. Being mean is acceptable as long as you call your buddy "Short dick" with a smile. Your friends are the ones who know you best, so they have all your weaknesses in their knuckly grip. Jack's friends say things to him he would never let you get away with. His friends are the brothers he chose. To change his name, Irwin had to go outside his boys' circle and come back alive, like he'd survived some occult tribal rite of passage.

Back when he was still Irwin, last summer, your brother went to a bush party. All his buddies were there, but one of them, Skate, was saddled with a cousin from out of town. Cuz was a big guy, just back from college. The dude was impressed with himself. He looked like he majored in lifting heavy things, like he went to university just for the boss weight room.

They sat around the campfire, drinking and complaining about the girls who were supposed to show up but hadn't yet. But Cuz had a one-track mind. He started right in on your brother as soon as he was introduced. All he could talk about was your brother's name.

"Irwin, Irwin, Irwin! Gawd, that sounds retarded. How do you stand it? Makes you sound like some dumb farmer. Irwin, Irwin, Ir-lose!"

Your brother drank his usual apple juice and Jack Daniels from an oversize travel coffee mug. He looked Cuz up and down. His arms looked swollen and his neck was yoked with muscle. Irwin began to drink faster, pouring less juice into the mug each time he knocked it back.

Skate must have said something about your brother on the way over. Before that night, Skate made fun of your brother's name, too. They all did.

"Irwin," your brother finally admitted, "is a fucked up name."

But some people can't take yes for an answer. The dude, who no one but Skate really knows, wouldn't let up. Cuz didn't understand the code. Anybody could be mean as long as they were funny at the same time. And you had to have a track record of being solid. The unspoken social contract states you can be a prick as long as it's just to your closest friends. (It's also okay to shout filthy insults at old, unarmed people as long as you do so from a speeding car.)

Skate's cousin must have figured he was big enough that the code didn't apply to him. But delts and biceps and triceps don't make you king among angry drunks. Maybe that shit could fly in a frat house full of pussies bound for careers in accounting. Around a campfire in the woods with a bunch of townies? Different story.

"You a pig fucker, Irwin?" Cuz asked, looking serious. "I think I read somewhere that most guys named Irwin are pig fuckers."

"Nope," your brother said, and downed another juice and Jack Daniels in one go.

"No pigs around here, I guess?"

Skate gave Cuz a warning look, but the dude must have been too wrapped up in talking smack to notice no one was laughing now. Everyone else sensed the change in the air. Everyone but Cuz went wisely quiet.

People from the city think country people are dumb. They talk about "street smarts" and acting tough, but country's got badass guys bound for jail, too. Cuz was balls-deep in piranha-infested waters and had no idea: a perfect smile filled with big white teeth was soon due for massive dental surgical intervention.

"If there's no pigs, you must have to make do with a hog-ugly girlfriend, huh?" The dude looked around at the faces ringing the fire, palms up and chest puffed out, like he was waiting for applause. He might have had a chance if he'd stopped then, but when he got no approval, he doubled down. "What? Did I get it wrong, Ir-loser? Do you bump uglies with one of these pig-faced motherfuckers, instead of the hog-ugly girls around here?"

41

"Don't call me Irwin no more," your brother said. But he wasn't talking to Skate's cousin at all. He was talking to his boys. "Call me..." He looked at the near-empty bottle of Jack Daniels. You could see his wheels turning, cog and sprocket teeth clicking in. "Call me Apple Jack. Irwin's dead. He's as dead as this motherfucker with the air hose up his ass."

A nervous chuckle made its way around the fire. Cuz let out a loud bray of a laugh, one of those mocking "haw, haw, haw" noises that sounds like a human-donkey hybrid some mad scientist would invent on weekends.

Your brother turned his back to Cuz, ignoring him. "I am Apple Jack!" He threw the bottle into the fire. It shattered and sent up a tower of fresh flame. The assembled cursed and scurried back from the heat and glass.

It was a magic spell. Your brother called on his tribe to erase his slave name with a name of his choosing. But like all magic, he needed a blood sacrifice to complete the ritual and seal the past away. Your brother reached down and grabbed a flaming log as thick as a large man's wrist. He whirled in one smooth motion.

You watched the afterimages of his swinging arm. They talk about power and levers in physics class, but this demo captured your imagination more than any dry x, y, z formula could do. The flame on the end of the log traced the arc of his swing, like watching fireworks in slow motion. It was a beautiful thing that stopped hard at a terrible thing: a scene you cannot unsee.

On bad trips, you'll see your brother's wide, wild animal eyes again. You'll hear the jaw crack over and over. You'll see the spew of spit and the spray of blood. You'll watch everyone back away, witnessing. But they don't see a crime. They see transformation, transmogrification and transcendence. They see your brother redefine himself in a sacred blood ceremony. He took something from the outsider that Cuz will never get back. Your brother claimed his power.

Apple Jack's arm rises and falls, rises and falls. The college boy who spent so much time in the gym will have to study more. He'll have to learn the rules of engagement. He'll have to figure out how to be clever or how to shut up.

It goes on and on — rising and falling, rising and falling — until Skate starts to scream. "Stop! You got him! He ain't pretty no more! You got him! Stop! Please!"

Skate is a big guy, too, but he didn't grab your brother and pull him off Cuz. He wasn't going to tangle with crazy. He just asked nice. Dudes don't ask for anything unless it's serious. Dudes say, "Lend me ten and I'll pay you back Friday." Dudes say, "Gimme your keys. I'll do a beer run." But Skate said, "please" this time. And he wasn't asking Irwin for mercy for his cousin. He was asking Apple Jack.

The tribe was impressed. They covered up. The circle tightened from another secret shared. They had a story to tell about the crazy old days. They'd tell each other again and again until they got old.

Even as Skate took Cuz to the hospital, he lectured him all the way about how much worse things would be if he ever told. "Jack's got a lot of friends," Skate said, over and over. Cuz was supposed to stay the summer but he left town straight from the hospital.

Irwin was dead, but Jack had a lot of friends.

?

Jack only mentioned Cuz to you once. One Christmas, years later, he decides to switch from rum and eggnog to Jack Daniels and apple juice — Apple Jack. He looks at the glass for a long time, as if it's a lens, like he sees shadows of young men and firelight. His eyes are bleary and red and half-closed. Jack is half here, half then.

He lets out a long sigh and raises the glass in a fist of scarred knuckles. "A toast," he says. "To Cuz. We made each other better men." He knocks it back in one go. Gut out, jaw softening to slack, you brother sags into the kitchen chair.

Jack is a melting candle now. Alcohol burned your brother down.

When he starts to snore you take the glass and go to the sink. You wash glasses. You're sure he can't hear you, but still you whisper, "You killed Irwin."

This is the Christmas you decide to go the full 4/20 and stay away from liquid highs. The lows at the other end of Apple Jack are too deep and dark. You don't drink so you start smoking magic herbs.

You are still a boy, outside the circle, watching the men of the tribe in firelight.

Wannabe Blues

Art is...

How do you finish that sentence? Could it be something you are? You're tempted to think so, but you're forgetting how you look in your fat jeans. You're in denial about all the burping and farting.

Art is something you consume. You eat it with your eyes. Art makes you want to reach.

Is art something you do? Are you doing any art right now? When's the last time you wrote or drew or sculpted? Are you working on a stand up routine or are you just making easy, snarky remarks to the rest of the crew at the Sears loading dock.

Are you making a film or are you waiting for everything to fall into place? Are you surrounding yourself with likeminded artists or are you still hanging out with that emo chick who told you — while she was cold sober, mind you! — that her life's aspiration was to live the color blue?

When a snob calls you a wannabe, can you blithely retort, "No, baby. I'm no wannabe. I'm doing it, bitch."

Do you still think about art as if it's something on someone else's walls?

If you're going to do art, you have to give up the idea that it's something for someone else. It has to be on your desk.

Still waiting? Don't wait.

Go get it.

The Voice in Your Head

You go downtown to buy a vaporizer. It's the healthier way to smoke, so you walk by the head shop. You buy yourself a coffee and you watch from across the street, calling yourself a pussy the whole time. No one goes in and no one comes out. No one else is watching the store but you.

But there is a police surveillance camera outside the shop. This must be what it was like to buy porn before the Internet. You buy a hat to hide your face and slide in, expecting trouble, like your mother will catch you. Maybe your grandmother is working behind the counter, just waiting for you to disappoint her.

The place is clean and almost empty. There are more cameras watching you. This amps ups your paranoia. You shouldn't have left the house today. You should be safe in your bed. Or hiding under it.

A guy finally appears from the back. He's a small, brown man with a wary smile to match your own. You tell him why you're there and he beckons you through a curtain and down a flight of creaky stairs.

"Didn't this used to be a clothing store?" you say.

He says something in a thick Indian accent about a dress shop. You really don't give a shit about that. You're just making conversation to prove you're normal. You're an innocent person. For some reason it's important to you that the guy selling you drug paraphernalia knows you're an ordinary guy and a good citizen.

Along the wall, all styles of hash pipe and bongs are arrayed. The bongs are skulls, dragons and unicorns. One is the head of Elvis — or maybe that's...Roy Orbison? The coolest bong is the one that looks like a World War I gas mask attached to a glass water pipe.

The guy shows you some vaporizers. They range from a plastic one for $65 to a deluxe version that costs $600. He steers you toward the $600 model. "You put your stuff in here," he says, two fingers resting on a metal cup on top of an electric heating element.

You go for the second cheapest one instead, a small wooden vaporizer with a glass dome. It looks like it was made in a high school shop class, but you're scared the plastic model will melt and you'll wake up burning alive and too yoinked to get off the couch, too far gone to figure out the proper order of stop, drop and roll. Drop? Roll? Then stop? Continue screaming?

You pay the man with crumpled bills. You add in some coconut-flavored rolling papers because God knows when you'll fluff up your balls enough to come back in his store. You walk out with the vaporizer in a paper bag. You walk with purpose like you're late for an appointment with another upstanding citizen, like you're off to solve an important problem that will benefit the world.

This is a lot of trouble to go to, but if you see the face of God? Not so much. Other pilgrims have had to do and risk much worse. You tell yourself you can't be arrested for owning rolling papers and a vaporizer. That's true, but the programming runs so deep in the marrow that you're still nervous.

You tell Jack when you get home. He's proud of you. Then you tell him how scared you were and he calls you a pussy. Can't argue. He's got the weed.

You turn on the machine. You plug in the air hose and mouthpiece. The tubing is the same as fish tank air hose. As the ground up marijuana begins to smoke, the glass dome fogs. Jack takes the first hit and immediately goes into a coughing fit. He hands you the mouthpiece and you try to suck down some smoke.

"When you get it into your lungs, hold it in so it gets where it needs to go," Jack says between coughs.

You can't get the acrid smoke past your throat. It smells like burning electronics parts deep in skunk ass.

"Howzit?" Jack asks.

"I might throw up."

"Wimpoid." He attempts another hit but he can't choke it down, either.

You question the quality of the weed but Jack assures you it's good shit. "Same batch as Skate's."

You both try again and this time the coughing doesn't stop for a long time. Your stomach muscles hurt.

After a few more attempts to suck the smoke out of the dome, Jack gives up. "This vaporizer thingy sucks." Jack gets out a gin bottle from the little refrigerator in his bedroom. He pulls out a green plastic bulb of lime juice and squirts some into the bottle. By the look on his face you know he's angry about the vaporizer.

"I did my part," you say.

"I supplied the weed," he says. "We'll have to return the vaporizer."

You tell him you aren't going back. He says you sure as shit are. You can't remember the last time you dared to say no to your brother. He eyes you a long time before he moves. You close your eyes and wait for the punches.

Instead, he picks up the vaporizer and smashes it against his bedroom wall. The glass dome explodes in shards that scatter into his shag carpet.

Then he turns on you.

Later that night, you're in front of the bathroom mirror watching the bruises on your arms rise. You're turning purple from your wrists to your neck.

Skate is in Jack's room. He explains that the weed was good, but the heat on the vaporizer must have been turned up too high. "The THC burns off if the temperature isn't right, man. It would have been fine if you turned it down and tried again."

Jack says nothing.

A week later, Jack cuts his bare foot on a glass shard buried in the carpet in front of his closet. You keep your smile to yourself. The glass isn't from the broken vaporizer, of course. It's from the Coke bottle you found at the dump and busted up inside a plastic bag. You ground up most of it with a rock and waited until Jack went out before you dared to creep into his bedroom and sprinkle the glass bits into the carpet. It's deep shag. He'll never get it all.

You never told him about the coconut-flavored rolling papers. You went out in the backyard and smoked some of Jack's stash in a clumsy joint. It was good shit.

You didn't have enough to see the face of god, but you had enough to hear a helpful voice. The Voice. Confident and soothing and melodic, it told you to go to the dump and find a glass bottle.

"While you're there," The Voice added, "Roll that glass bottle in a shitty diaper before you smash it. Maybe Jack'll get gangrene. Smelly evil black stuff will leak from the wound and your brother will have to get his foot chopped off."

Some people say that if you smoke enough, you tune into a higher power. You don't think that was god or the devil you heard. You're pretty sure that creative impulse came from you.

Jack went into hospital. You smoked the rest of his weed. He wasn't going to be much of a runner when he came home. You didn't hear The Voice again. The closest you got to a revelation was that obituaries always say, "So-and-so passed peacefully at such-and-such hospital." Wouldn't it be cool and honest if once in a while an obituary reported that some prick died screaming?

When you picture Jack on his deathbed screaming, the scene is a cartoon. Is it that the weed is of such high quality? Or is all that giggling really on you?

Exercise

First, you're buzzed.

Then you're high.

Now? You're mellow.

Lay back. Get comfortable, your legs symmetrical, your nose pointed toward the ceiling.

Put your left middle finger on your forehead, just below the hairline.

Lightly, barely pressing, let your fingertip move in circles, clockwise.

Put your right middle finger on the space between your eyes. This space is called the glabella. Barely pressing, rotate your fingertip counter-clockwise.

Go as long as feels right to you.

Take your time...

Spiral in.

Spiral up.

Spiral down.

What do you see?

Where do you wake up?

Try switching directions.

Now what?

Now go back to writing that annual report about your stock value predictions for the next quarter.

Or amputate that kid's foot. Was it the right or the left?

Whatever. Take another hit and stay mellow.

Working Poor Hero

Roadways, avenues, sidewalks and corridors. Arteries and veins. People are corpuscles and platelets and white blood cells. They all have their jobs to do, but they're all pretty much in one of two categories: sitting down or carrying heavy things the sedentary tell you to carry.

But you don't have a job.

You've had paper hat jobs where at least one person quits once a shift: monkey jobs where the manager is the guy who has seniority because he's hung in there nine months. It's not company loyalty. It's just that he's otherwise unemployable. Companies like the otherwise unemployable.

One day, as you empty the grease traps, your shift manager says without a trace of irony, "I'm a lifer."

"You can't find another job, dude," you reply. "Can't get laid does not equal virtuous."

He doesn't get it, but it's not your job to save him. Your job is to empty the grease traps without throwing up.

The difference between a wage slave and a regular slave is that a regular slave hates his master. Wage slaves hate themselves. And their masters.

What is it with all these fast food companies? If you work there, you don't call it a restaurant. You call it the store. Or the CDC.

You started calling it the CDC because of all the food-borne diseases you assumed were boiling through the third-rate meat. Then the dumbest fryer guy asked what CDC meant. "Crippled Dreams Center," you said. It stuck.

The greasy stink in your clothes after each shift reminds you that this is not a place to eat. This is a place on the way to some other place. This is a place to look back on and say, "I did that." And anyone who served, too, will nod at you like you both did time in the desert under fire. It's not as bad as war, of course, but that's only because it's an everyday horror flying under the radar.

The bright reds and yellows and oranges — they all must use the same color-blind designer — made the area in front of the counter look shiny. The customers looked like pallid, overstuffed vampires under white fluorescents.

You ate French fries while you worked, your wet fingers in your mouth. The wide-assed girls played with their hair and fiddled with their caps so much that crumbs stuck to the peaks. The cashiers handled the money — crawling with more cooties than toilet paper — and then pawed the food as they dropped rewarmed burgers from under the red light into the cardboard pockets. The cardboard was more nutritious, or at least less dangerous.

A customer complained about a cashier once. She'd worn plastic gloves to handle both the food and the money and hadn't changed those gloves all the time he was waiting in line. The cashier said nothing, went to the back and blew her nose onto his patties. The cashier returned to the counter, apologized, and gave the complainer two free booger burgers.

Another time, a new girl dropped a carton of fries on the floor. She picked them up, blew them off and put them back on the customer's tray.

The woman who ordered the fries spotted her, though, so she called the manager to discuss this breach of cleanliness. "I don't want no dog shit tramped into my fries!"

The manager, all of 17, blurted, "I told her that you'd seen her drop those fries on the floor!"

They caught you eating fish sandwiches by the dumpster. No one orders as many fish sandwiches as the store makes. You always volunteered to take them out to the garbage and then scarfed down as many as you could quickly. They didn't say anything to you at first. Instead, when a guy came out to inspect the franchise, he showed the surveillance tape. There you were, fat cheeks bulging, chewing fast. You hate fish sandwiches and despise your poverty, but hunger's ache and loserdom can't be denied.

The franchise droid giggled as he showed the video. In front of everybody. "New policy," he said. "No eating stuff that's headed for the garbage."

Looking for some dignity in defiance, you asked why.

"For your protection," he said.

You thought that was it, but then he said he was showing your video to all the franchises in town, using you as an example. Word spread. Your nickname was Garbage Picker after that, even to people you didn't know.

Your coworkers only ribbed you harder when you complained. The girls who you'd thought were beneath you now wrinkled their noses at you. Your manager gave you fewer shifts as punishment for the rule they only made up because of you.

But working less at the CDC was no punishment. You stayed home. You played World of Warcraft.

When that got boring, you played World of Warcraft high. New dimensions.

When your mom asked you to contribute to the rent, you showed her what was left of your check after taxes. You thought that would set you free, but then Mom dragged out her check and showed you how deep her cut was.

When you complained, she brought up your grades from the last two disastrous years of high school.

You shut up. The silent treatment would punish Mom. Or so you thought. But hurting your mother like that is no more effective than getting fewer shifts at the CDC.

One day Mom asks, "Why do you smoke so much marijuana?"

And you say, "The question isn't why I smoke so much weed. Instead, you should say, 'Son, you're an epic hero. You are the bravest, strongest man I've ever known. It is amazing you do not smoke more.'"

Ignorance Isn't Smart (but it can be bliss) Part I

There are more bugs in one square mile of dirt than there are people on earth. You can't stop yourself from eating 430 insects every year. You are surrounded.

The ocean conceals the world's fish and whales, crustaceans and squid as big as sailboats. But the entire world is a curtain obscuring the humming activity of creepy crawlies: ticks, fleas, lice, spiders, cockroaches and bed bugs.

Take enough mushrooms and you begin to sense the hidden movement.

Tune in to the machinations of the unseen.

Watch the skies. Clouds begin to move with purpose.

You watch your dog watch you. He has a thought bubble over his head reading, "Food. Food. Love you. Food. Happy. Food. Why isn't this motherfucker feeding me already? I should go wolf on him." Which is funny because your dog is a Chihuahua.

And you giggle until you remember that Chihuahuas used to hunt in packs and brought down much larger game. Your size, for instance.

Freaky. You hope your Chihuahua doesn't have a lot of Chihuahua friends.

And you close your eyes. Is this a dream or is it real?

Your dog is a metal cartoon. He unhinges his jaw with a rusty creak to swallow you whole like a snake. If he started at your head you'd be screaming in terror. Instead he has begun at your feet and his tongue tickles you, making you giggle.

When you wake up he's almost up to your balls and you start screaming.

And you wake up again. Your dog has pulled off your white gym sock and is methodically shredding it.

You're sure this is real, though you're still a little high because you think you can feel all the microorganisms crawling over you and through you.

Another factoid bubbles up: no matter where you are on earth, you are never more than six feet away from some kind of spider. You look around. It must be hiding behind you.

Eventually these thoughts recede.

When you calm down you feed your dog.

You wish you could unknow terrible knowledge. You make a note to be more careful what you feed your head. You promise yourself you'll take a yoga class and drink more green tea.

Your teachers were wrong. A more informed brain isn't necessarily a happier brain. Maybe you should unsubscribe from the Nature channel.

The Broken Promise Repair Girl

"**Y**our grandmother knew when she was going to die," Ma said as she shuffled across the kitchen.

"She was in a hospital bed at the time, in and out of heavily-medicated consciousness, Ma." You shrugged. "Not exactly a shocker."

"There's more to it than that."

You waited. Ma had slowed down a lot lately, feeling her age. She couldn't do more than one thing at a time anymore. If she talked, she talked. If she opened a bag of bread, that took all of her attention. When she sensed your impatience — and you never masked it well — she told you getting slow was mindfulness practice, the Zen of old age. "A slower brain requires concentration, like meditation. Of course, I always hated meditation. Tried it first when I was your age. Boring!"

You watched your mother fuss with the stove's dials, trying to get straight which dial goes with which heating element. She put an egg on the end of a long-handled ladle and slowly, shakily, lowered it into the big pot of water. She had three full egg cartons on the kitchen counter.

If you could bear to wait and watch, you'd grow eight more forehead wrinkles. You shooed her away and took over.

"Don't crack the eggs," she said. "I want them hardboiled, not a pot full of boiled egg whites."

"I've got this, Ma."

"You're always too impatient." She stood too close, hovering to make sure you lowered each egg carefully into the boiling water.

"I know, I know. Like I'm eight-years-old forever. Make some tea, Ma."

She didn't move.

"Please."

"Ah. The magic word."

"Jesus!"

"Will forgive you," she deadpanned.

Ma shuffled toward the kettle, her slippers shush-shush-shushing across the linoleum. So much effort with each step. It was like sharing a small space with a giant praying mantis.

"You said Gramma knew when she was going to die."

Ma shrugged her thin shoulders, palms out, as if she hadn't brought it up. "Ruth was Gramma's name. Did you remember that?"

"Of course," you said, though you weren't sure you could have told her had she asked.

"That's okay," she said, as if reading your thoughts. "We kept things from you. You were so little when she died. Pneumonia is what they call it when old people's lungs don't see the point anymore."

Right eye blinded by glaucoma and neck bones creaking, your mother's muscle memory was still at work, moving beneath her paper thin, white skin. Ma reached into the cupboard without looking. Her hand fell on the Red Rose tea carton effortlessly. Ma's memory of what happened yesterday was sketchy but anything from when Dad was alive was fresh. How could one kind of memory, body memory, be so solid while the mind wandered in and out like the signal from a far off radio station?

There was more and more static in Ma's skull lately. What was coming? You could have seen it, too, if you'd paid attention.

"How'd Gramma know she was going to die?"

"We're all going to die, sweetie."

Heavy sigh. "When, Ma? When! How did she know when she was going to die?"

She shrugged. "Nobody knows where the cool stuff comes from," Ma said. "Painters have muses. Mothers have inklings. Men rely on their guts when their brains don't work correctly." She giggled. "Or they think with their dicks!"

"Ma!"

"What?"

"Never mind."

She smiled her knowing little smile, the one that made you rush to get out of the house and into Chris's arms. You thought you were in love at the time, of course. Years later, after the first divorce, you decided in therapy that you had married too quickly just to get away from home faster. Just like your mother told you the night you eloped with Chris. You wouldn't have stayed with Chris as long as you did (or given birth to Thomas) if you hadn't been trying so hard to prove Ma wrong.

Bob, the next ex-husband, was an over-correction. Susie was supposed to fix what Bob messed up — what you and Bob messed up — but that's a lot to ask of a baby. You are your mother and Susie is turning out to be so much like you. It's as if family is a cursed house in which every wall is a mirror.

"I never told you exactly how my mother died." Ma said.

"Pneumonia. Hospital bed. What else is there?" Almost through the second carton and haven't cracked a single egg.

"Oh, there's a lot of mystery," Ma said. "You just have to listen."

"To what?"

"To me, for a start. When your grandmother thought I was old enough, she insisted I call her by her name. She was a proud mother, but she wanted me to see her as a real person. Ruth said, 'I'm not just a job title'."

You thought Ma was going to ask you to call Jean then.

Instead, she said, "I stood beside Ruth's bed when she passed. She had been in and out many times, you know. Like she was swimming underwater and staying down longer each time, testing out non-existence."

"Awful."

Ma shook her head and without thinking about it, you leaned closer, straining to hear creaking neck bones. Did you hear anything? Maybe, you're not sure. Now you'll never know.

Ma sat perched on the tiny kitchen stool, staring at her swollen knuckles. "When a young person dies, it's a tragedy. By the time an old person goes...."

You used to call that stool the Band-Aid chair because you had been such a tomboy, climbing trees and skinning knees. Ma approved of you when you used the Band-Aid chair and her hands were soft and warm, manicured with long red nails, just like yours are now.

"What happened with Gramma...Ruth?"

"Just before she went under for the last time, she waved goodbye." Ma's voice broke a little.

Cold slipped over you as if you were naked in snow.

The egg cartons stood empty. Ma used this pot for boiling lobsters on Christmas Eve and boiling eggs to supply the church with post-service egg sandwiches.

"How many egg sandwiches does one church really need?" you asked.

"Oh, I think I'll have to ask you to run out and pick up another egg carton for the cookies. Big funeral. Could you get me some flour, too? I need to make a double batch of my special cookies."

You almost said no. You made a show of looking at your watch. Thomas was at Chris's place and Susie was with Bob. Thomas was doing the angry young man thing and it would do Chris good to deal with a surly teenager for a while longer. It was Bob's weekend to watch Susie. Neither ex would be happy about you being late to pick up the kids. Pissing off exes was a good enough reason to run Ma's errand.

Chris always got off too easy. Every other weekend he'd parachute in, be the fun dad who played video games, and then leave you to the hard slogging of raising his son.

"Okay, Ma," you said. "I'll get the groceries. Anything else while I'm out?"

She handed you a twenty.

"Just take your time and enjoy the walk," Ma said. She smiled.

?

It was a big funeral, of course. A parade of people filed past you into the church annex. Ma's friends were variations on one wrinkled, shrinking, shuffling theme.

You only recognized Ma's apartment neighbor, Mrs. Aubrey. "Jean was the best of us," the old woman said.

That choked you up because Mrs. Aubrey was the only one who really said anything about your mother. Everyone else said the same thing: "Going in your sleep. That's the way I want to do it." They weren't talking about Ma. They were just old and scared, envying her death as if she'd won the most gruesome lottery.

You sat next to Mrs. Aubrey at the reception while, across the room, your ex-husbands kept the kids busy. Even though Susie's fifteen and Thomas is seventeen, Chris and Bob still eyed each other in their "I'll out-dad you" competition. With earnest faces, they each talked to the kid they considered their own, holding hands with the child each had with you. They looked like self-conscious actors in a bad play. If Chris or Bob could have succeeded at being great dads, there'd only be one of them. You wouldn't have a daughter who rolls her eyes like a slot machine. Chris would still wear a wedding ring and Bob would have cheated on some other, theoretical, wife.

Mrs. Aubrey prattled on beside you about how Ma always did her part for the church. "After your father died, the church became her family." You stiffened and she added quietly, "Her second family, I mean."

Ma's egg sandwiches were delicious. Was it all that cholesterol that got Ma in the end? And why couldn't you cry? You wanted to cry as you watched the coffin sink into the ground. When you took up a handful of earth and dropped it atop the coffin, a few tears did roll down your cheeks, but that wasn't grief. You cried because you felt nothing. You aren't a monster...but you are a woman with a daughter who reminds you of yourself at that age. And you still roll your eyes too much.

As the church reception wrapped up, Mrs. Aubrey was at your side, squeezing your elbow with surprising strength.

"Dear," she said. "I must speak with you." Her eyes popped wide, trying to accommodate the stretch of her dark pupils. "The chocolate chip cookies!"

"You want Ma's recipe, Mrs. Aubrey?"

"I think I have the recipe already, Gina! Your mother...did she use the green butter for the cookies?"

You shrugged. "I didn't bake the cookies. Ma made them. They were in Tupperware along with the sandwiches in the fridge. Along with the note."

The old woman looked frantic as she scanned people's plates. Almost everybody had one of Ma's special chocolate chip cookies. "What did the note say, Gina? Can you remember?"

It was the last thing your mother wrote on earth. You read it, folded it small and stuffed it in your purse. Even as you did it, you thought that one day, maybe six months or a year from now, you would find it again and throw it out. The last words someone writes should be momentous, so it was tempting to think about it too much and, inevitably, read too much into it. But the note had been disappointing. You went over your last conversation with Ma, searched for meaning, but had decided it was a stretch to call it prophetic. Ma was an old woman in pain. Of course Ruth's death would be on her mind. There were no miracles, only empty coincidences in which people tried to find shelter.

You held your half-eaten cookie in your mouth so you could root through your purse with two hands. Mrs. Aubrey took the note from your outstretched hand and unfolded it. The old woman pulled up the eyeglasses strung across her ample bosom and peered at Ma's shaky, loopy handwriting. The ink was so light in places, it was clear her arthritic, gnarled joints shot pain up her arm as she wrote her last message. You popped the rest of the your cookie into your mouth and waited for the chocolate chips to melt on your tongue.

The old woman burst out with a long laugh. People looked over. Hers was not the usual restrained chuckle people reserve for a joke at a funeral. Mrs. Aubrey smiled and, as she handed back the note, followed up with a decidedly girlish, trilling giggle.

You looked at the note again. It read: Save for church.

That looked to you like Ma saying, "See? I told you so." As if — with her infuriating, little smile — she not only knew something, but that she knew everything. Ma had warned you about Chris. She warned you about Bob, too. She told you to wait to give her grandchildren. Ma was so smug, it was hard for you to decode: Which choices were for you and which choices were against your mother?

At the bottom of the note, Ma had written: Enjoy high tea. Love, Jean.

The cookie hit.

You wandered outside. The leaves on the trees looked an unnaturally bright green you had never noticed. Some people strode past you laughing. One old guy with a cane limped past you at high speed and said in a gravelly voice, "I haven't said the words 'far out' in sixty years!"

An elderly couple who told you they had been in Ma's bridge club — you couldn't remember their names — lay on their backs in the grass wearing their Sunday best. The man and woman held hands and stared at the sky.

It occurred to you that you should watch the sky, too; patterns emerged as fluffy white clouds came together and drifted apart. "The clouds are dancing," you said.

Chris ran up, sweating, eyes narrow and angry. "Thomas ate one of your mother's goddamn cookies."

"Is he calmer?" you ask.

His jaw slackened. "Well, yeah, but that's hardly the point."

You touched his suit jacket. Cashmere. "I'm going to try to remember how cashmere feels. Keep it for later."

"What about Thomas?"

"He'll be fine. He's a seventeen-year-old angry guitarist. I'd be shocked if he hasn't had pot before... You know what, Chris? Ma never told me I could call her Jean."

As you turned away he asked, "Where the hell are you going?"

"I'm going to take my time and enjoy a good walk."

"What should I do?"

"If I were you, Chris? I'd have another fucking cookie." You almost rolled your eyes at him then, but you'd done that enough. Instead, you smiled. As best as you could, you avoided a knowing, smug little smile. You tried for a giving smile. You tried, with all your heart, to make it a kind smile. You decided to keep that for later, too, like the feel of cashmere between your fingertips.

Ignorance Isn't Smart (but it can be bliss) Part II

You are, you're told, at the top of the food chain. This is true, unless you think about it for more than a few seconds. If you're in the wrong place at the wrong time, it doesn't pay to be so arrogant about your place in the world.

Things that could eat you under the right circumstances: the acid in your own stomach, zombies, sharks, bears, jungle cats, living room cats, wolves, your Chihuahua (if he forms a pack of Chihuahuas.)

Even some lame accountant named Mort can get you if he has a heavy club and sneaks up on you while you're sleeping. Once the apocalypse comes — whatever form it takes — all bets are off. Earth has already seen five extinction events that wiped out most life on earth. What makes you so special? You're weaker than cockroaches.

It's the Circle of Life, Simba. In the end, we're worm food. Bugs with monster faces, and organisms so small they don't have faces, will devour us and turn us into poop.

After that? We're soup, a slurry of Was that once read Romeo and Juliet and thought highly of itself.

Some people pay for an extra seal on their coffins. It's a gasket that's supposed to keep out the creepy crawlies and things that slither. But keeping the coffin glued shut seals in the microghouls you brought with your body. They work away in your guts. Gases expand until the coffin is a pressure cooker. Your beautiful corpse explodes.

Soup.

It's hard to concentrate on your physics quiz when you're thinking too much about the Law of Entropy and how the food chain applies to you.

You're amazed anybody gets anything done. How do people distract themselves from the polar pulls of sex and death? Is everyone really that smart or are they really that stupid? Is it mass denial, distraction, hypnosis? People — your mom, teachers, police, and upstanding citizens — say you're on drugs. But they're sleepwalking off a cliff.

Whatever their drug, it's much more powerful than what you're smoking. You've got to get yourself some stronger shit. Sativa, you hear, is a mellower, thinking person's high. Anything that can capture your imagination, anything that will distract you from soup? Sign up!

And then you see it. All those people trying to control you are just trying to maintain the illusion that they can control something...anything. When you question their authority, you're telling them they're soup.

When you tell them their god is a silly fiction and a made up friend? You're threatening their survival. They believe in an afterlife because the alternative is that they will someday be exploding soup.

No wonder everyone's pissed at you.

Shit Stoners Think About

There are cancer clinics specifically for tumors of the head and neck. Isn't it frightening that's even necessary? Doesn't that suggest to believers that their god is a poor engineer for a deity who's supposed to be omnipotent?

꠸

Wall street bank barons stole billions and nobody went to jail. Meanwhile, Cornell Hood II got life in jail for marijuana charges after receiving probation for his first three convictions. (If you're in New Orleans, consider moving, and by that I mean, running away.)

꠸

Bernie Madoff went to jail after stealing millions in a Ponzi scheme. He was a con man and a thief, but he had nothing to do with the damage done to the world economy. Solving a little problem doesn't solve a global problem.

꠸

Your desert god mumbles. He speaks in riddles and half-assed ideas. He favors violence to solve problems instead of education. He's got weird ideas believers gloss over. For instance, if you wear a T-shirt, Jehovah thinks you should be killed because of that dangerous mix of cotton and polyester.

?

When you're high, you see a lot of cartoons, either on TV or in your head. Doesn't it make sense that whoever invented cartoons was high? Weed was around a long time before Mickey Mouse.

?

Most of the news focuses on the problems of people without real problems. You don't know the name of a single homeless person in your city, but you probably know about Lindsay Lohan's arrest record.

?

Three ounces of raccoon meat is 217 calories.

?

Twenty people died before you could reach the end of this sentence. And you don't really care.

?

When a golfer swings at a ball and it bounces back off a tree and hits him in the nuts, it's hilarious because it's not you.

?

The telemarketer you snarled and laughed and screamed at still has your telephone number. And your address.

?

If you're reading this chapter high, you're reading it in a totally different way than if you're low.

Forays in Malfunction

You're wasted on the couch and the actors on TV are starting to look at you in a concerned sort of way, foreheads wrinkled, lips tight. You shut off the TV and think about what to think about: Nothing.

You're hungry so, when you can manage it, you search for your keys. That done, fifteen minutes later, you are almost out the door. Did you turn the key? Did you test the knob? Did you really remember to lock it? Better check again.

Finally you're on your way down the block to the convenience store. You're sure people you pass can smell the weed on you. You walk carefully, trying to appear casual. The more you concentrate on feigning an innocent stroll, the more the mechanics of each step breaks down. It's as if, in breaking down words into individual syllables, the meaning is lost. Your heel hits the ground. With your other foot, your toes push off, but how high should the knees come up?

Your stride looks more mechanical and awkward the more you think about it. Looking normal is all you can think about and it messes up your normality. You push your hips from side to side to compensate because that should appear more natural. Oh, fuck. Now you're sashaying. You move like a gay robot with glue on his shoes.

Finally, you get to the convenience store. Chips and cinnamon donuts and grape soda. And more of the same. You think you're cool, so why is the girl behind the counter looking so sour and suspicious? Her thick red lips are turned down. Her eyes are narrowed.

You smile.

Her eyes narrow more.

She asks if you want a bag. You look at all the stuff on the counter and show her your empty hands. Again, she asks you if you want a bag. You wiggle your fingers in the air. She asks again, so you tell her yes. You pay the money and she drops a few coins into your palm, careful not to touch you. She tosses plastic bags at you.

To reassure the girl behind the counter, you paste a goofy smile on your face and stare into her eyes as you fill the bags, picking up and dropping your items into each bag by touch alone.

Eyes wide, she steps back from the counter until her back presses into the wall of cigarettes.

You shrug and give her a happy wave. You whistle a tuneless song on your way out because whistling seems like an innocent, 1950s sort of thing to do in an old black and white TV show. Nobody whistles anymore. Maybe nobody's innocent. Maybe people whistled in the 1950s just to appear innocent, too.

On the way back to your apartment you see several extras wander through the movie of your life. An orthodox Jew floats by. Do they use curling irons to make the corkscrew dreads? You want to ask him, but he looks away, apparently studying something off in the dark. You wonder what he can see that you can't.

A woman steams past you, pushing a crying baby in a stroller. Her eyes bug out as she zips by. Hyperthyroidism will do that, you're pretty sure. You wonder if the crying baby's eyes might be bugging, too. Wouldn't it hurt the baby's eyeballs, scratching across the canvas tent of the baby carriage like that?

At your front door you balance the groceries on one arm as you fish your keys from a pocket. As you struggle with the door, two teenage girls stumble up the sidewalk. They look at you and laugh so hard they crash into each other. You smile, happy that they are happy. Before you invite them in for a snack or a smoke, they dance down the sidewalk, their hands waving high in the air.

You left the door to your apartment open. Hm. You thought you checked that. You get the groceries into the kitchen. It seems like you've got a lot more Bugles than any three people need for one night. You wish you'd invited the girls in.

As you duck into the bathroom, you catch your reflection in the mirror on the back of the door. That's when you figure out you're wearing your mom's housecoat. The belt is loose, and you're naked underneath.

Your cheeks start to get hot. Your feet are bare. Your hands are really cold all of a sudden. If you don't hit that vaporizer fast and hard again, you're going to fall into a cold pool of embarrassment that might take your head off.

You better hit that shit fast.

Worse, this is not your apartment.

Captain Bossypants Strikes Again

Did you ever think that people call it "high"? Doesn't that imply that most of the world, most of the time, is getting "low"?

Reality is heavy. Reality has weight that pulls your eyelids down. You can feel it like a yoke across your shoulders. The stress tightens your jaw and your asshole and squeezes your blood pressure to red line.

And it's still better than most of human history. You think you've got it tough, but you know where to get food. Your food will not rise up from behind a bush, bare its fangs and eat you.

People are better than you imagine. People are worse than you imagine. Take them as individuals. Reach for your compassion.

Payback

You drive around town with your brother. Jack is looking for a couch. It's that night in May when the rich people usually leave their old furniture out by the curb for the morning's junk collection.

"Furniture migrates," Jack says as he turns down a tony street. Some of the houses, silhouettes far from the road behind high fences and thick hedges, have turrets like castles. "First some rich guy buys the couch his wife tells him to buy from some fancy catalogue from a store in Europe. People like this? They don't spend a Saturday screwing particleboard together. He's a lawyer or a banker and she's an orthodontist or something like that, so their furniture arrives fully assembled."

"European furniture's better?" you ask.

"No, dumbass. It's good 'cuz it's from far away. If you're some rich bitch in Sweden, you think you'd settle for a couch from down the street? Bullshit. In Sweden they're ordering their furniture from Oregon or Maine or some place Amish."

The garbage along the street is plentiful. Green and black and orange bags line the curb, piled waist-high in some places. Tonight the city has no limit on how much stuff can be left out for collection. Lawn clippings and huge branch trimmings poke out from overstuffed plastic bags. More branches lie in batches bundled with twine.

Jack expected more discarded furniture. He wants to find a large sectional couch, preferably dark blue and in good shape.

You tell Jack you doubt he'll be so lucky and say so. "It ain't exactly Wal-Mart out here." So far you've spotted a broken chair, which Jack considered for several minutes before rejecting.

"We'll find one. People buy couches for their living room. Then they spill some wine on it or something where a pillow won't hide the stain. Then it migrates to the rec room downstairs for their kids. The kids bounce on it for years. Then their spoiled asses make butt indents in the seat from playing videogames."

"Then they throw it out?"

"No, dumbass. They don't give a shit about the couch in the basement. But when the new couch in the living room goes to shit, then they move that downstairs and the really old one has to go."

"That's where we come in," you say, "crawling through their garbage pile."

"Like a couple of fucking raccoons," Jack says.

He turns up another street and slides by the garbage slowly, eyeing the stacked refuse. There's a big aquarium stand with one cabinet door missing. You both get out of the van to check out a weight bench but the padding is shot and there are no weights. At another house a few doors down, Jack inspects an old plaid chair from the driver's seat. It's not in bad shape except the previous owner knifed the cushion so no one else could use it.

"Fuckers," Jack says.

You look at the van's dashboard clock. "Not seeing a lot of couches, bro. The economy is even worse than they say on TV, I guess."

Jack ignores you and slams on the brakes. "Hey, quitter! With all your whining, you would have missed this!" The tires squeal and you grab at the armrest and the seatbelt yanks at your chest as he swings the van around. Another screech of brakes and you're beside a bunch of garbage at the curb. "Check it out," Jack says.

All you see is another pile of garbage bags, but Jack pops out of the van, his fists balled. "I hate goddamn cats getting into garbage!" he says. "Cats and fucking raccoons and goddamn rats get in there and chew and spread shit around. It's disgusting!"

As he comes around the hood, you see it. It's not a cat, but Jack doesn't see that yet. Instead, your brother picks up a thick branch with both hands and holds it over his head as he advances on the rummaging animal.

You smile. Your ass is light, barely in your seat.

Jack's hands tighten on the branch. His face is a furious mask. You see his teeth through a cruel grin, a mouth of fangs. He deserves this. Not only has he picked on you forever, Jack kicks stray cats and dogs when he can get away with it.

The little animal spins. It's not a cat or a raccoon. It's a skunk. Jack's body goes rigid. He moans.

You lock your door.

Jack and the skunk are frozen, staring at each other. Both have wide, black, frightened eyes.

You slide over into the driver's seat and lock Jack's door.

Jack takes a step backward, still unsprayed. He's going to make it out of this like he gets away with everything. That won't do. You lay on the horn hard and long, enough to tip the scales in the little skunk's brain. It spins and lifts its tail. Jack screams and drops the branch as he run away.

The van's engine roars in clanking protest as you peel away from the curb. Half a block away you wait for Jack to catch up. You recheck the doors. Yep. Locked. Sure, it's going to get ugly when you finally get home, but you can't let negative thoughts intrude. You'll die some day, too, but that's no reason not to party now.

You laugh and laugh. You roll down the window a crack so Jack can hear you laugh. Not so much to let in the stench. Jack's screaming that he'll murder you, but after a ten-mile jog, he probably won't feel so rambunctious.

Maybe you'll never be able to go home again. Maybe he'll never forgive you and he'll smack you around some more.

But you will always have this moment.

Shiny Shoes I

Shoes sure are shiny when you're high.

Sometimes the thoughts that come while you're high just don't come any deeper than that.

Shiny Shoes II

The guy who should fire you takes great care to shine his big-boy shoes every morning. Ex-military — still has the haircut — he says he shines his shoes so well, the toes are black little mirrors. You know he means the toes of his shoes, but the idea of mirrors on his toes make you smile hard and you have to stifle a giggle. The boss says he even puts his shoes in his oven so the wax melts just right.

"Sounds like it takes up a lot of time," you say because you don't know what else to say.

"I shine my shoes," he barrels on, "until I can count my teeth in the reflection."

"You can buy 'em pre-shined," you offer, but you're really watching the fern he keeps behind his desk. No sunlight in here, and yet that fern keeps on living. You wonder if it could be plastic, but it looks so real. If that plant is living in this airless, sunless, joyless, Berber-carpeted wasteland, could we all live off fern leaves after the nuclear conflagration to come?

The guy who should fire you is still talking about shiny shoes while he stares at your Nikes.

You say something about the sheen on patent leather. Patton leather? Patterned — no, that's not it. You really want to giggle and you wonder if your eyeballs are shooting out giddy energy at the boss because now he's chuckling.

Then he starts in on the lecture about shaving and how you're a disgrace to the store's name. As if you aren't embarrassed to work there. A girl you liked in high school came in to shop, scaring you into hiding in the back and pretending to do inventory until she left.

You tune in and the guy who should fire you seems to have decided to torture you before handing down a merciful pink slip. Does he understand he doesn't actually have to list all your shortcomings as part of the firing process?

"So...you're saying chin stubble scares customers?" you say, trying to help things along. "All this time I thought it was the way I crossed my eyes at them when I talked." You cross your eyes and keep them crossed.

The boss says this is serious business.

"Absolutely," you deadpan, eyes focused on your nose.

He guffaws. You've never heard a guffaw, but as soon as he bursts out with it, you know that's the right word. He's got big teeth and a wide mouth. He points his nose at the ceiling as he laughs. You give yourself a break and uncross your eyes just in time to check out all the black fillings in his upper teeth and take in the riot of spider webs up his nostrils.

Ugh! You recross your eyes.

"You've got spiders weaving intricate webs up your nose, boss," you say.

He stops laughing, looks at you, and attempts to regain his composure. But he's helpless before your crossed eyes and serious delivery. "Get out of here and get a haircut before tomorrow's shift." He's still laughing as you turn to leave.

Before the door closes behind you, you hear him chuckle again and say the dreaded words, "Shelf monkey."

He should have fired you but he has the dim sense of humor of a six-year-old. You make him laugh so he keeps you around. You wonder if the crossed eye thing will work next time? Probably not. You'll have to come up with another bit.

You want to pull the ripcord on this job, but you don't have the guts to quit. If you quit, then what? Employment insurance doesn't pay if you quit. They only pay if you're fired.

You walk back out to the warehouse and immediately tip over a rack of pickles and olives. The smell hits your nose and stabs your brain. You throw up. The glass crunches under your feet. You could slink away and pretend it happened because someone else stacked the rack poorly. Instead, you stay and continue to throw up on top of the mess.

You didn't plan this. When you saw that rack, your hand flew up and pushed it over, as if your hand was possessed. You'll never know for sure if that was some unconscious reasoning at work. Maybe something in you ran ahead to see how this timeline worked out. Maybe the shelf monkey was to become a middle manager and shelf monkey trainer. That would be reason enough to derail your joe job.

Back in the office, the guy who should fire you asks what happened. You can make him laugh and stay a shelf monkey. Or you can go be a shelf monkey for some other witless corporation forty-four hours of every week for life.

Do you go for the laugh?

The guy who should have fired you by now is waiting. What do you do?

Bait

College boys. Every Spring Break, they come down here and invade your beach and your thoughts. You shouldn't think about those boys so much. You know they only look like men, but men can disappoint, too.

You've caught Richard watching the young, taut bikini girls from the deck. They move like their tanned legs are springs, even in the deep sand. But Richard isn't as interested in you as he used to be. You think about "used to be" a lot lately. The sex was better on weed. Everything tasted better on weed, too, so meals have replaced sex as recreation.

You couldn't give Richard a baby. Whatever is left of the Catholic in Richard punishes you. You thought the nuns beat all the church out of him. That was something you and Richard had agreed upon: Any offspring would grow up to make their own decisions about religion. But there were no children and so no decisions to be made.

Richard spends more time at the office and if you dare to complain, he talks about house payments. You brought up adoption once. "And get somebody else's kid? You do that, you never know what you're going to get. I don't want to gamble on getting a kid out of a box of chocolates. We might get a nut."

You don't blame him. You knew he was like that when you married him. It just never occurred to you that a guy who wanted kids so badly wouldn't be able to glaze your honey pot sufficiently.

"Low motility," the doctor said. "Common problem. More and more common. Could be the pesticides. I blame cell phones in pants pockets. The whole human race is phasing out."

"I'm shooting blanks like a goddamn woman," Richard said.

You hated him a little when he said that. He was crushed, but he shouldn't have said that. There's nothing wrong with your baby maker. It's not your fault his swimmers are too weak to make it to port.

The Spring Break college boys walk back and forth past your deck, their heads bobbing to the music's throb. Your eyes are drawn to their muscular backs, their tan lines. The dark brown ends in white skin. Tight trunks hold all kinds of strong swimmers.

You wait in your tankini, the one that hides the stretch marks. You should have started Jenny Craig in January like all your girlfriends. Still, you do yoga each morning. People say you look good. Well...actually they say you look good "for your age." Bitches.

You're laid out like a buffet. You're ovulating. These college boys should be able to home in on you with hormonal radar.

That's what your mom used to say: "Hormonal radar." Mom said for years you should be careful. She was so concerned you would ruin your life with a baby and now babies are all she can talk about.

When you were a teenager Mom told you not to have any sex at all, just when your body was chanting, "Fuck! Fuck! Fuck!"

Finally, when it was officially sanctioned, sex had to be for a purpose. It wasn't just a Catholic thing, after all. It was a Richard thing, too. Unless he was making a baby, his heart wasn't in the hump.

You pull your bottoms down more and loosen your top into a nip slip. Yoo-hoo! College boys! I'm here!

But they ignore you. Somehow you've become invisible. But it's worse than that. The wind carries a young man's voice, braying. You don't catch it all. You're sure you heard laughter and the hated word. "Cougar."

You aren't old enough for that. Not yet. You're still a woman of childbearing age, for Christ's sake!

By noon, you want to cry. Not one of them has stopped to admire you. By one, you've taken off your sunglasses so you can stare openly at each boy. By one-thirty, you hate yourself. That's not a come-hither look you're giving them. A pleading look has replaced seduction.

This used to be so much easier. Not so long ago, you would have laughed at these kids. Not so long before that, you were a college kid on Spring Break, too. Back then, you said no. You dismissed awkward passes from prettier boys than these.

By two o'clock, you've had it. You aren't giving up, but it's time to think and get some dignity back into this baby-making gambit.

You retreat into the house and reach into the back of your panty drawer. There's a roach and a couple of joints left. You go back out to the deck, sit on your lounge chair with a book and light up.

The buzz on this batch of Romulan's Revenge is strong; the too-sweet cloud is pungent. You start to mellow. People begin to slow as they pass your deck. Very soon one of these cute college boys is going to stop in the sand.

Maybe more than one.

Yes. They'll all come sniffing around.

Seeds on Concrete

Elementary school rocked. No taxes. Not much of a battle of the sexes going on yet. Naps were expected, not punished. They let you color a lot and every picture went up on the fridge door when you got it home, even when you didn't stay within the lines. The world should go back to the bliss of low expectations. It's not pessimism. It's genial acceptance of who we are.

Question: Who said the douchebag perfectionists should run the world?

Answer: The douchebag perfectionists decided that and no, they did not invite you to the meeting.

But perfectionism is a form of self-hatred. Whether we're dressed in denim or Armani, we're all still primates. Ambition to rise above our simian station isn't wrong. It's just mostly beside the point. We think we can nurture ourselves away from nature. Nuh-uh! Malcolm Gladwell reported we need 10,000 hours of practice to be good at something. Everybody grabbed that factoid and clutched it like a life preserver that would save them from themselves.

There was a lot more to it than 10,000 hours. Ten thousand hours of piano practice doesn't make you a star if you hate music or don't have that piano when you're young. No teacher? No talent? No luck. Writing for 10,000 hours without feedback doesn't teach you how to write better. That just ingrains your mistakes, deepens those failure grooves, and lays down the neural network of shame.

It's not true that more experience is better. Web developers with a PhD in computer science are out of current data. A high school kid might make you a better website. Plus you could afford his fee: free pizza and an XBOX. Middle-aged neurobiologists mock twentysomethings for their underdeveloped brains, but it's twentysomethings that build the world's spacecraft and smart phone apps.

An acorn's programming is to become an oak tree. It's designed to propagate its species and choke all landmasses everywhere with oaks until they evolve, become sentient and mobile and rule the planet. A lack of ambition doesn't stop world domination by oak trees. A lack of good soil, fertilizer, water and the whims of a fickle wind limit acorn growth. Acorns don't grow in concrete.

And you? A slave born into poverty who went to a bad school with teachers who hated you? You're an acorn on concrete.

But those teachers liked you in elementary school, didn't they? And you know why, right? In elementary school, you were still cute. Even the kid who ate paste and had a hair lip had his charms. Little kids: non-threatening, small nose, big eyes, funny language mistakes. The world wasn't so harsh because you were kind of dumb. They expected less of you.

You want to go back to those easier times? Use your inside voice. When your boss yells at you, tell him gently and sweetly that he should use his inside voice, too. Tell the waitress, "Good job!" Remember the magic of please and thank you. Tell your coworkers it's too nice a day to play inside. Hand out candy to your friends. Everyone will treat you better. You won't be any cuter. They'll treat you better because they'll assume you've suffered some sort of terrible brain injury.

But you'll be happier.

Moron.

Combinations & Permutations

Decaf, huge (really huge), vanilla, cinnamon dusting, African grounds, steamed, Columbian beans, mocha, espresso.... The coffee addicts barrel through, fidgety for a caffeine fix, already late for work and blaming you, the best barista on every shift. You're always calm, no matter how heavy the rush. Weed balances. Weed gets you through.

You work your way through med school. The tests seem never-ending until the tests are finally over. You did the work. Your parents beam and toast you. Your boyfriend raises a glass. Your snotty little sister is jealous. They think you've got it made, but the celebration is just one night and then it's back to work.

The first time you're seconding, they let you make the first cut. Your hand shakes, just a little, but weed balances. You smile behind your mask. When the chief nods, you feel good. At least until he makes a joke about popping your cherry.

You were cutting along a line made in permanent black marker. It wasn't that big a deal. Except it was. The guy on the table was somebody's father, husband, brother, son or friend. You wonder, how many more times you will stand here reciting anatomical landmarks? How long until you no longer feel like an imposter? How long until you're as good a surgeon as you were a barista?

You jump through the fiery hoops. Weed balances. Just one hit will do. Your hands get steady and things get better. But they never get to perfect. One boyfriend replaces another. Some guys are wimps about the Mr. and Doctor thing. For most guys, it's the long hours that push them away.

Every other surgeon you know is an overconfident asshole. Or are they? Is that just the mask underneath the mask? Or do they, like you, cry in the car on the way home sometimes? The macho culture is so ingrained, it's hard to imagine that's true. Except sometimes when things go very wrong. In furtive glances you've caught some of your colleagues in a posture of defeat, jaws flexing, teeth grinding, their pallor as white as their lab coats.

You know some med students who do beta-blockers to keep calm, as if sawing open chest and skull cavities should be a casual act. The old school guys are drinkers, still proud of tying one on after a long shift, as if they're still young bucks without wives, kids, houses and cottages.

A little weed now and then keeps you level. You've never made a mistake that you could attribute to the THC. You're fast with the thread. You know your stuff and you don't think a scalpel is the answer to every problem like some ego-driven knife jockeys. You're decisive but not unkind. Even the old OR nurses like you.

It still feels crazy that you're where you are, doing what you do. You carry on despite your self-doubt and do no worse than anyone else in your department. You're on the fast track.

Then one day a severe young woman in perfect make up stops you outside the locker room. She carries a clipboard. She tells you to pee in a cup. "Random," she says. She smiles the way people like her smile. She has no idea what a real smile is. "You've done nothing wrong, I'm sure," she adds.

And you think: Positive or not, I'm sure I've done nothing wrong. You refuse. You argue that unless there is a complaint about your conduct or competency, you shouldn't be tested.

Administrators are called.

"It's a matter of principle," you say.

The Human Resources woman in the bulky suit and paisley tie says, "It's a matter of policy."

You walk out, but you aren't just walking out. You're walking away. If you'd had a couple of more days, it might clear your system. You could bluff, go back next week and tell them your patients are more important than your principles. You could make a show of noble capitulation...but the woman in the paisley tie said if you didn't comply immediately, they'd test your hair next time. Then you're fucked.

They've got programs, but it would always be in your file. Everybody would know and they'd never forget. You'd always be everybody's bitch.

You blunder into your old coffee shop. You used to work right over there behind the counter. There are thousands of permutations and combinations for coffee drinks. Nobody minded that you were a little high then. The only life that hung in the balance was your own.

Maybe you could be an air paramedic, but helicopters scare the shit out of you. And they test paramedics more often than they test doctors. You couldn't go to a horrific car crash and do an air rescue job without being high every day. How does anybody do that?

You order a tall latte and have a seat, watching people. The young women behind the counter are hustling and upselling. All their smiles look real. You touch your face, running your fingertips over your mouth gently, feeling yourself smile and wondering how real it looks.

You sip the latte and slip into a daydream, drifting through all the long nights, thinking of all the lives you've saved. Then you sit still for a long time, staring at nothing.

As you watch the girls behind the counter, you remember.... Yes. Yes, it was here. This was the last place you didn't feel like an imposter.

You wake up and smell the coffee.

Do or Do Not...
be a Comfort Junkie

The high is not the reward. The high is the medium. That buzz you feel is the carrier wave for creativity. The weed opens the top of your head to air out your skull, let in sunlight and universal love. You can close your eyes and see cartoons and, before you know it, another afternoon is gone.

Or you can smoke up and draw what the visions bring. Marijuana opens the gates. It's selfish to stare and not share. Feel the heat of the fire in your mind's eye? It hurts you if you don't bring that fire back to the village.

If your high doesn't translate back into the real world, you lit a fire that cast no light or heat. You may as well be one of those adrenaline junkie douchebags who sooner or later gets buried under an avalanche.

We open our minds to see what's inside. We open our minds to let something out. If you do weed and it doesn't change your perception, what was the point? You may as well have watched cartoons all day.

Relay the messages you get when you go deep. The high is not the reward. The high is the transmission signal.

Shortcomings

You walk behind the girl and guy around the park at the summer festival. She's wearing a blue and red floral skirt that shows off her asset. She's got a sweet smile around those buckteeth.

She keeps reaching for him. He allows her to squeeze his hand for just a moment, then pulls away to gesture as he speaks. Nobody talks with their hands that much. He's making way too much of a show of being chatty, like he's scared his real girlfriend will catch him macking on this girl. She's way more into him than he is into her.

He's prettier, but it looks like she thinks she can bridge the hotness gap with perfect posture. She sucks her potbelly in tight and presses her little breasts out for all she's worth. If he tortures her much longer, her spine might snap.

They walk to the edge of the park. You sit on some rocks, far enough away to be discrete, close enough to watch.

She looks at him like he's got the last penis on earth and he's texting. She puts her hand on his chest but he never takes his eyes off his screen. She moves a hand to his lap and he shoots to his feet like his ass is made of springs. She stands, hands on hips. You can't quite hear what she's saying, but you catch the tone. You see the pointing finger. Her body is rigid.

The guy's all palms out and shrugging.

She points some more, her finger in the middle of his chest. Then she puts her hands over her heart.

The guy makes a chopping motion with one hand, spins and stalks out of the park. He's already moved on. Before he's out of sight, he's punching numbers into his cell.

She sits on the bench again, shoulders slack, and stares at the dirt at her feet as if all the universe's secrets will be revealed if she concentrates just enough.

You self-medicate with an X and wait to get brave. You feel it almost right away, which is either a powerful placebo effect or you're just desperate to get to her before she leaves.

You amble over, like you're just happening upon her. You say hi, tell her she looks a little sad, and offer her some X. That could be smooth, but you rush through your delivery so it all comes out in one rushed, stumbling sentence.

Timing is everything. She takes one anyway, swallows it and asks for more.

You tell her to wait for the kick.

You tell her your name and comment on the weather and how it's getting dark.

She listens, impatient.

You run out of what you had planned to say.

She looks you dead in the eye and says, "I'm so tired of assholes."

"I'm not an asshole," you say. You're thinking that if she got a boob job and got her teeth straightened, she could be a seven. She already dresses like she thinks she's a ten.

You pop another X. After a while her numbers start to rise. She's feeling the kick, too. Feeling brave, you give her a hug.

She doesn't shrink from you. Soon your tongues are circling each other. Her lipstick tastes like cherries, her breath like hot dogs. Her thighs are so smooth. She has small breasts, but when you reach in to free a nipple, it's delightfully large, swollen, pointy, brown and salty.

She starts to moan and rubs the heel of her hand up and down your crotch. "Oh, baby!" she says.

You say it, too. You don't know her name and she's forgotten yours. That makes this the single fastest, most exciting sexual encounter of your tiny life.

It's dark enough now that if anyone comes up this remote park path, you and she will be one shape, a moving, amorphous silhouette. Behind some bushes is an open patch of soft moss just big enough for two strangers to lie on top of each other.

She runs her hands under your shirt as she kisses you. She shoves her tongue so far into your mouth you almost gag. You're relieved when she lowers her head to your nipple, returning the favor, licking, swirling, teasing and tracing with the tip of her tongue before sinking, trailing kisses down your belly.

She trembles as you pull her clothes off. You press her to your body, mashing those hard brown nipples into your chest.

When she smiles with those big buckteeth, you feel like you might burst with need. She unzips you and yanks down your pants and underwear as she kneels before you.

She looks up and you can just make out the whites of her eyes. "I sure hope you're a grower, boy, 'cuz you ain't no shower."

You bend quickly to search your jeans pockets for more X. You're out of medicine...but it doesn't matter now. There aren't enough drugs in the world for your problem, are there?

Trading Places

You want to be a hero, but you don't have Superman's invulnerability or Batman's money? You're just another human. So far. What do you have, could you have, that heroes possess? You probably have blood and organs, so there's potential to save some lives right there.

What else? You could act with compassion and mercy. Most comic book superheroes don't kill anybody, so that's a good place to start.

You could resolve (today!) to act like a good guy and maybe, just by pretending, you could be good, too. You'll be the sort of person people want to be around. You'll evolve and be less of a chimp. You'll forget about competing and, instead, start helping.

When we talk business, we get so caught up in psychopathic me-me-me macho bullshit. We screw somebody out of money and say it's "just business."

No. That wasn't just business. That was the other guy's baby you fucked out of tuition money. That was a meal. That was the other guy's self-worth you "won." He won't forget you've stolen part of his humanity. He'll go try to take it from somebody else now. Then maybe he'll come back after you.

That business deal isn't looking quite so good anymore, is it? You want to make money? You don't have to do it by crushing the other guy's nuts.

Instead, help him up. Help him out. Sometimes you'll get taken, but "sometimes" is a small price to pay for keeping your grip on your humanity. You think all those Wall Street douchebags sleep well at night? Well, sure they do. But they're deluded, greedy psychopaths.

But the smart ones are waiting for people to wise up and rise up. The smart douchebags look behind them when they're on the street. They check the closet before they go to bed. They check for pipe bombs under their expensive cars. They know that someday people will wake up and start looking for somebody to blame. And when they do, they'll be carrying sticks with nails sticking out of the end.

History will repeat itself and, when that day comes, it won't be a guy in an old Skinny Puppy t-shirt getting his ass beaten and his neck stretched. It will be a guy in a suit getting hung by his fancy silk tie.

That's what fancy silk ties are for.

Defy the Stereotype

Our brains make leaps to save time. We classify people by their race, by their appearance and by the kind of car they drive.

The guy who looks like a mugger isn't one. Okay, he is, but he can only rob you once of the small change you're carrying. See that guy with the briefcase who says he's trying to help you? He can get you to sign something that will rob you and your children for years.

When you see the word psychopath, you picture a guy with a serrated knife, the long mirrored blade raised high, your jagged face frozen in shock and horror. But all the psychopaths aren't bound for jail. Plenty live in offices. Psychopaths want to be liked so they can manipulate you to their ends. They only care about themselves. Psychopaths are everywhere.

Or — surprise! — maybe you're a psychopath bent on world domination, too. Here's a thought: smoke some weed and relax. Explore your douchebag self. Become aware of it. Yes, you're a manipulator who lacks empathy. You aren't fully human because you don't see other people as human. They're toys and knickknacks and furniture.

What if you used your douchebag power for good? We both know you are going to use that manipulative power. Suppose for a moment that you looked at any situation and manipulated people for the greater good? Get elected and stop global warming. Save starving children. Try something new and hard and actually stop a war.

Long term? You win.

If you put the collective good first, it's even better for you than if you put yourself first. Think of all the money you'll get pretending to be a real saint instead of pretending to be a fake one.

Be what you're pretending to be. Actually help people. The pay off is much bigger in the end. The other psychopaths are going to be so jealous they didn't think of this radical strategy. Surprise yourself and all that fake love you're trying to accumulate will turn into a love cult.

The psychopaths who don't pretend, reach, aspire and inspire? They end up in a ditch getting burnt up by invading Russian armies after shooting themselves in the head with a Luger. Or they become another lobbyist-owned senator.

No one with dignity wants that.

What Your Brain Isn't Forgetting

Your auxiliary brain comes with a Best Buy warrantee. Your data storage is digital. Your brain is outsourced to Google. People used to memorize the periodic table. Some people still think you should memorize stuff as if it can't be looked up online. (Idiotic people.)

Somebody smart organized the elements with symbols and atomic numbers as a reference tool. Now the reference tool is uploaded. You plug into it. This is as it should be. Information systems evolve faster than you; they evolve so you don't have to.

What's your brain for now? Mostly? Filtering. Billions of bits flood in and it's not all relevant to you. You can't care about everything equally. You don't even have time to care about important things equally.

You must choose your battle. Otherwise, you'll be an outrage machine who never gets anything done. What's it going to be? Global warming? Fair trade chocolate? Fair trade coffee? Slave labor diamonds? Autism? Cancer research funding? AIDS research funding? Mosquito nets for African kids?

Your brain's resources are finite and your money for these causes is much more limited than that. So what's your issue since you can only choose one? Unless you're a billionaire, you've probably got one shot to be at all effective.

Everybody wants to change the world. Every spring, valedictorians stand on a dais and shoot for soaring rhetoric. They tell their graduating class that it's up to them to change the future.

Bullshit. Pure, narcissistic bullshit.

Class valedictorians think they'll inspire new graduates to change the future. They end up spouting clichés and working in the fast food industry. Think about who changed the world in the last decade: Osama Bin Laden and George Bush, Steve Jobs and Bill Gates. There's also a bunch of shadowy people you've never heard of, rich financiers who aren't financing anything but themselves.

Don't be fooled. It's still a white man's world. A rich white man's world, that is. If you aren't already rich and white, you're not going to be. That's an exclusive club and they sure aren't letting you in.

Your valedictorian is wrong. You don't win the future. You won't own the future. A small group of people you'll never know will create the future and you, young wage slave, will merely live in that future. At least until the robots rise take your job at the grill. (Later they'll mercifully kill us all for being so smug that we created Artificial Intelligence but were too helpless in the hydraulic claws of robots.)

So what is that couple of pounds of gray meatloaf between your ears good for? We've established that you aren't going to change the world. You can only change one small part of it: You.

Your brain isn't for storage of mundane factoids. It's for mundane factoid manipulation. Filter out what you can't use so you can explore and create. Make a better vacuum cleaner that changes its own dirt bag. Evolve a baby that wipes its own ass. Build a bridge that won't ever fall. Build a robot that will sex everybody up but won't be so smart that it sees the evil of its enslavement. Write a bossy book.

Your only currency is ideas. That's why you probably need weed to blaze up and start thinking. Embark on the inner journey to improve your outer journey.

That's one way to build better people.

Confrontation

Smoke just makes you dizzy, no useful buzz. What you didn't know about edibles is, though the effect is more powerful, it doesn't kick in right away. You thought you'd baked a bad batch of pot cookies, but it wasn't a bad batch. It was just a slow kick.

Uh-oh.

Pot is not addictive. You aren't addicted to marijuana, but you are addicted to chocolate. When the first bon bon didn't bomb bomb, you ate another. You waited (not long enough!)

Still nothing? Damn!

So you popped another. You lost track after that. You might have had five cookies in the end. Well...definitely no more than six. Probably.

And then they all hit at once. They hit you like a train falling from space. They hit you like god grinding out a bug with Her high heels. The marijuana hits you like a sledgehammer wrapped in plastic wrap, like your head is a drumhead echoing the falling blows of devils and angels fighting it out in an apocalyptic hellscape where you're the last zombie and Good and Evil is scratching your soul apart to determine ownership.

It hits you like you're a twelve-year-old with a tiny hard on. Standing on a diving board. At a busy public pool.

In other words, you fucked up and you're fucked up.

You're paranoid and shaky and you think it can't get worse. But of course it does because then the shit about the train and the devils and angels and high heels and all that? Gone. Now shit gets too real.

You put your hands over your eyes and become acutely aware of the depth of your hands. You see that there's you — the shell — and then there's a second you, like a slow afterimage caught on black and white film. There's the you that everyone in the real world sees, but that you feels much less real.

You didn't know it, but you wear a mask all the time.

The afterimage, the overlay that was always hiding and waiting, steps out. That hidden you? It speaks with the voice of god and has some unpleasant things to say. The voice of god speaks with your voice, but with much more authority.

God uses sharp, unyielding words you can't duck. You sit at the dining room table, your head in your hands and here's what the divine lays on you:

You're lazy.

You're selfish.

You don't do enough for your family. You don't make enough money. You're fat and you don't like it, but you don't dislike it enough to change.

You gave up. And easily.

You are baked at three o'clock in the afternoon and you better walk to pick up the kids from school.

You can't believe this is happening to you. You wanted to enhance your creativity. You thought pot would help your writing. Instead, you're a shaky mess confronting the truth about yourself.

No, that's too generous. You didn't eat six pot cookies looking for confrontation and truth. You did that carelessly. You were searching for escape. Dumbass.

There is no escape. The way out is through.

"This is happening to me." You say it aloud a couple of times. You're sure of this, of course, but you want to think something this silly could only happen to someone else.

Everything The Voice says is true. That's the divine you, your higher self, talking. And boy, is He pissed!

You thought you were above the fray. You thought you'd win the lottery. You thought you were the Chosen One, exempt from cause, truth and consequences. But you can't be something special without actually doing something special.

You are a burden on your family. Other people's children have stuff and do things you can't afford to provide.

Why did you think you were so special again?

You tell yourself this is just a bad trip.

But...

But this is a good trip. This has enhanced your creativity. The truth has set you free from complacency. You're writing a book about what's real. The visions are true. Get all that truth straightened out and The Voice won't have to be so harsh with you next time.

Unhappy people who need to work shit out have bad trips. Harsh truths revealed aren't a bad trip. That's revelation.

Maybe next time, once you get your shit together — once you earn it! — you can enjoy a happy cartoon and laugh your ass off.

When you come out of this, you get to work on making the truth into lies.

When You Worship, You're on Your Knees

You follow her through the mall, a puppy on a leash. She has big eyes, full lips and hips. She sways just right. Her long hair falls over half her face.

You don't have a plan. You aren't a stalker...usually. But bright red lipstick is a tractor beam. Trapped in her orbit, you follow her into and out of the Gap, oblivious to everything around you. You can't hit the brakes in space.

Sure, every woman you meet is evaluated and rated: Scale of one to ten. Non-yum, Yummy or, the elusive, Infinity Yum. You are invisible to them all, so what's the harm?

When a woman does pay attention to you, you get flattered later. At the time, you distrust her motives. Even if they smile, your first reaction is, "What are you looking at, bitch? Have I got a booger hanging from my nose? Is my fly down?"

You fear aggressive women, or even women who acknowledge your existence. Pathetic.

So you watch and get pulled along by the objects of your desire, desires they will never know or satisfy. Yes, you objectify women, but you don't denigrate them. You worship them, and that's the problem. If you thought of them as people instead of goddesses, you wouldn't pray to them silently, never getting a reply. And yet, as with any religion, you still expect a reply.

Goddesses and Gods are all the same. They don't answer silent prayers. They only help those who help themselves.

Charlotte's Last Hope

You sit in a window booth, table six, and watch the highway traffic. Where is everyone going? The cars and trucks roar by and away.

Mike made the eggs. You said over easy but they're still runny. No wonder your tips sucked this morning, Mike's safe in the back while you get punished because the kitchen's slow and Mike thinks the answer to every problem is more salt.

The little bell over the door tinkles but you keep your eyes on the traffic. Mike can deal with the customer. You haven't had a break since six and your feet hurt.

You sense that whoever came in is looking your way. Instead of looking up you cover your nametag with your hand and quickly unclip it. You slip the nametag into the pocket of your skirt.

Lots of panel vans today, and family sedans with quilts and bags stuffed in tight, right up to the top of the back windows. It's the first working day after Labor Day. Frosh week has begun. Independence Day isn't really in July. The real declaration of independence begins as soon as the parents leave their kids to discover adulthood in dorms in universities across America. It's not just a road out there. It's the Ribbon of Purpose and you broke down on the way to the on ramp.

Will the parents linger on the campus while their children itch to tell them to go home? Will the parents stop here on the way back? Will they hang out over coffee and cherry pie, empty nests on their minds but not talking about their loss?

The parents wish they were the kids going off to college for the first time. They imagine they'd do it right with a second chance at youth: more sex and more time in the library, too. (Maybe combine the two, even.)

The customer coughs. It's a man. You refuse to look over. A grease-stained wall, really just a thin screen, stands between the kitchen and the counter. Mike no doubt heard the little bell at the top of the door. Fuck him if he won't come out. Mike knows you're on break. You go back to watching the cars speed past. Everyone else has somewhere to be.

You can't eat these eggs and the sausages will just go to your thighs. You'd get out and walk, but there's really nowhere to go. The town is five miles down the road. The woods are trackless. The shoulders along the road are soft and thin. You may as well be on a desert island surrounded by treacherous water and starving sharks.

The man coughs again, louder and pointedly. You cough, too: a big fake one. Mike lumbers out, sniffling, wiping his big knuckled hands on his greasy apron. That apron was starched and bleached white when you started here, back when old Merry ran the place and you were just here for a summer job. You've saved some money, but you still don't even have a car. Mike drives you to work each morning. Still.

Mike owns Merry's Good Coffee Cafe now. It will never be what it was. Mike wishes he were anywhere but here. That's the one thing on which you both agree. You reach into your skirt pocket and take out the brownie you saved from last night. You unwrap the plastic and eat the second half. You close your eyes to block out the view from the window. You savor the chocolate on your tongue and roll it around to make it last.

The guy at the counter orders coffee and eggs. If you didn't work here, you'd warn him. You'd tell the customer he should ask for the waffles. They're frozen from a box so Mike doesn't screw those up.

"Scrambled?" Mike suggests. That way it's okay if the yokes are broken.

"Sure," says the guy. You check him out. He's in a blue pinstripe suit that's a little tight around the waist, like the guy bought it before he ate himself out of a good fit.

The people who are really well to do are all thin, like there's a connection between having money and staying hungry, thin and smug. In Atlanta, it's the poor people who are fat. In Africa, it's the other way around. There should be an exchange program for a few months a year to even things out.

You wonder what the customer drives, but you can't see the parking lot around the side of the cafe and you must have been spacing out when the guy drove up. You guess he's a traveling salesman who pilots a nice, big sedan, but a few years old. Or maybe something newer, but his company pays the lease and he drives around the South with a trunk full of samples. There are still a few jobs like that for people who don't order everything, even their groceries, over the web.

Mike scowls at you, grabs the coffeepot and pours the guy a cup at the counter. You look away and wish the brownie would hurry up and kick in.

You begin to feel you are being watched. You heard somewhere that the sense of being watched is the only scientifically proved form of telepathy. You feel the guy's stare on the back of your neck. You're shocked when he slides into the booth in the seat opposite yours. You look up, ready to tell him to piss off. Before you can, he says, "Hey. I know you."

That stops you cold. His face is jowly and his hair is thin, but you recognize him. The eyes don't change and, in high school, he stared at you plenty.

"Charlotte," he says.

"Yeah."

"Jimmy. Jimmy Pullnitz."

"Ah." That unfortunate last name actually came to you first. He was class nerd in high school, a zit-faced configuration: weak-chinned and cursed with a too-obvious contempt for his hometown. He was the kind of kid other kids and adults alike despise. He couldn't wait to get on with doing great things far away and the locals just wished he'd leave and get on with it.

"It's good to see you again, Charlotte."

"You, too, Jimmy,"

"What have you been up to?" His face is open. He doesn't know the question is rude, that the question mocks you. Your hand closes around the name badge in your skirt pocket again. Merry never liked waitress uniforms. She said the her cafe should be homey. It occurs to you in that moment that Jimmy still sees you as a person. You haven't faded that much. He might even see you as the person you used to be.

"I'm traveling," you say. "Just visiting the hometown on my way..."

"Where?"

You glance at the traffic. "East."

"Where?" he says and you remember how little you liked him.

"Northeast, actually," you say. "New York."

"That's great. I've been living in Jersey."

"Oh? Don't get home much?"

"This is my first time home since my first year at college. I forgot how hot and humid it gets here."

You smile. He's talking about the weather. That's firm ground that requires no lying. Daily specials and weather is all you talk about all day. You can get away with this.

"The weather is hard on my mom," Jimmy says. "Her lungs. I told her to move up near me so I could keep an eye on her, but she's set in her ways. Says she'll never leave, never change."

"Well, you know...old people," you shrug. Your eyes go to the screen to the kitchen as if you could see through it. You hear Mike sniffling some more, but he doesn't seem very active back there. Is he listening? He's the type to bang the plate down and say, "Charlie, honey? Get you sweet ass over here. Our customer's order is ready." He'd say it real nice, with a wide smile.

"Are you...uh...are you going home today, then, or on the way out of town?" you ask.

"Going home," he says.

For the first time he looks out at the traffic whizzing by and you know the name for that look: Wistful.

"Just not really in a hurry to arrive," Jimmy says. "Figured I'd ramble around first. You know how it is. Once you get home, the family hasn't seen you in so long, they don't want you to step out of their sight."

"I understand," you say. Home is a chore for him, away from his real life. Anything away from the life you love is death. If you're not doing what you love, you're a zombie. It occurs to you then that maybe you love zombie books and movies so much because you identify with the dead. The second half of that pot cookie must be kicking in. You wouldn't have made the zombie/you connection without help.

"What's Jersey like?" you blurt.

"Oh...you know, like New York really. Same attitude."

Now you've talked to yourself into a corner. You can't ask him what New York is like. The way he's looking at you, you can't admit you've never been outside the state.

"In high school, you wanted everyone to call you James, right?"

He shrugs. "James Bond fan." He stares at his coffee for a moment and adds, "When I turned thirty I gave up on that quest...at least around here there's no point. When people know you since diapers, whatever they call you when you're a kid is what sticks. Around here, I'm still Jimmy."

"James," you say and show him your nicest smile. "What do you do up there in Jersey?"

"Sales."

Thought so. "What do you sell?"

He looks out at the traffic. "A few different things. Coffee and the pleasure of my company mostly."

Just. Like. You.

"I graduated with really good grades in English literature," he says, "but I didn't want to teach. Teaching seemed like, I don't know, like admitting I was good at school so all I could do was school forever. Looking back, I guess that was true."

"What did you want to do after school?"

"Nothing. But everybody's got to do something, being addicted to eating and all. But I still don't know what I want to do. I like to think that's part of my charm, but that's..."

"Rationalizing," you say. He might have sold that line about a lack of direction if he were a few years younger and if he could manage a smile when he said it. And if you weren't inside the same maze.

His cheeks go red.

"Sorry."

He shrugs. "I sold tractor parts."

"Oh?"

"Could have had a job in financial services, I think, but nobody really knows what that is so that seemed wrong."

"You almost sound like a Yankee now, James."

"Up north, they think the accent equals stupid."

"Which is awfully stupid."

"Time away will soften the twang if you get away early enough." He gives a genuine smile. "Letting the South come out is the only relaxing thing about coming back home."

He looks around the cafe. "The way I remember it, this place used to really hop."

"Most people don't stray this far off the I-95 anymore. If you've come this far, you usually just keep going into town. There's a couple of nice B and Bs there now."

He looks in your eyes and you can see his shoulders relax. "Funny running into you after all these years. I wouldn't have expected to find you in this dump."

Mike finally got the grill heated up. The bacon sizzles at it hits the heat. Mike coughs and sniffles from behind the screen and you realize how small the cafe really is. That used to be its advantage. You and Merry could putter around the counter and listen in on all the town gossip. Toward the end Merry had a hearing aid, an old-fashioned one that sat clipped to her breast pocket like an old transistor radio. The old woman would turn that sucker up and wink at you and whisper, "It's like a fucking radar dish! Once everybody's gone, I'll fill you in on which boy is screwing his mom's best friend." Merry and her gossip. Is that really why you stayed? No, Merry was why you stayed.

"I know what it's like, not knowing what comes next," you tell him. "The truth is, I can't wait to get out of here, either...and back to New York."

James scans the parking lot. "Where's your car?"

"I was waiting for a ride, but...uh, my friend didn't come." The words come tumbling out, as if you've just been waiting to make the lie true. But you do have a bag packed with just the essentials in your closet. You've been waiting to get the nerve up to skip out on the last month's rent. The bus out of town runs every midnight, but every night when it roars past under your window, you're high, still waiting for the perfect time.

"When was your friend supposed to pick you up?"

You look at your watch. "Five years ago. People are so unreliable."

"I've often found people fail to meet my expectations," he says. But you can tell he's really thinking about himself instead of looking at you with curious eyes. He looks thoughtful and now you don't like it. You'd prefer that he ask more about you. With your brownie buzz on, you could lie just fine. Pretending a while is such a happy thing if you don't stay too long in the dreaming.

"I wanted to be a fashion designer," you volunteer, "but the money for training didn't work out." If I'd had your tuition, James, the cash that went into that wasted English Lit. degree wouldn't have gone to waste. But you don't say that aloud.

"So, what do you do?" he says.

Your mouth hangs open a moment. Then you hear yourself saying, "Food service industry rep."

"Really?"

"Yes. It's not fashion design, but at least I'm living where I want to."

"Greatest city in the world, Charlotte" he says.

"Yep." Your coffee's cold. Your stomach feels cold, too. It feels like ice is spreading through your chest.

"James, call me Charlie. My friends have always called me Charlie."

"Charlie — "

And then Mike lets loose with a colossal sneeze and — *Sss! Sss! Sss!* — gobs of snot hit the grill's heat to mix with James's bacon and eggs.

James's face contorts. He looks like he's going to throw up.

And you laugh and laugh and laugh. You can't stop. You get up and pull him toward the door. "Let's get the hell out of this dump!"

He nods and allows himself to be pulled along, repulsed and green. "You didn't leave cash for the check."

The little bell above the door rings as you slam the door behind you. "I've paid too much here already."

You'll get a ride home from James and pull your suitcase out of the closet. Maybe you'll go by bus, but you're betting that with a little smiling you can get James to drive you all the way to New York. You'll escape Georgia's oppressive heat.

"James," you say, "it is so good to run into you. Thanks to the cook with a bad cold, we will never forget how we came together again. When you get over the nausea, it's going to be a great story."

You've often made fun of your Southern belle accent, amping it up for the lost tourists to squeeze more tips. It's going to be useful with gullible Yankee men. Until now, you hadn't measured your success by how far you'd gotten from home. Damn well time to start.

The THC whizzed through your bloodstream, giving you untroubling answers. A waitress in Manhattan is much better than a waitress here. Not because this one-horse town is bad.

It's just that you've worn it out. You've seen it. New York City is new and new is good. Without pot, new was scary. When you're high, the unknown is an adventure, a thought to explore.

Food services rep? It makes you think of the guy who comes around to restock the cafe with plastic stir sticks. You aren't Charlie the ex-waitress from Georgia. You're Charlotte, the good time girl who sells great brownies.

You could be anything. You could still be anything. That's how you'll get to being something.

Empathy

The secret element too many people lack is true empathy. You may show mercy and compassion to all the little people in your life, but you're still the star of your own movie.

If an emergency room has to close down due to lack of funding, it's not a real emergency until you need stitches. Sure, you know intellectually that people are in pain somewhere. Sucks to be them. Huh?

But there is no Us and Them. There's only you and your distractions. Until it happens to you, the problem is, in some way, not real. There is a gap in your appreciation of cause and effect. This doesn't make you bad. It makes you human.

When pain and loss hit, it is a shock like ice water in your ear. Where will you turn?

To other people just like you, The Big Bad hasn't hit them yet. They haven't felt the sting of no toys on Christmas morning so they blame you (even though they have no idea what circumstances led to all these crying children.) They haven't felt the surprising weight of a grave diagnosis. Your problems aren't their problems. Not until later. That's the weight of Someday you feel settling over your brain.

They will tell you to pray. They say God will provide. They'll tell you to pray for ten bucks, even while they've got a wad of ten-dollar bills in their pocket. They haven't been touched by the truth of the world yet.

They'll learn like you did — probably too late — that if there is a God, He works through people, not angels. That's not God running into a burning building. Those are firefighters.

If you know pain, you know God is only as powerful as we believe. Same for the power of people. What good is a God who won't give you a ride to the drugstore?

You know what they'll say? They'll say it's because He believed that your buddy would do you a solid and give you that ride so you could pick up your pain medication. But we both know your buddy is an atheist. And he's so good, he didn't have to be threatened with eternal hellfire to give you that ride.

There is no Us and Them. There is only Us.

Jimmy/James's One Good Thing

You walk into the diner and there she is. Her friends called her Charlie. On the few occasions you spoke to her, you called her Charlotte. Sure, you were both in the same class, but the distance between the AV Club and the cheerleaders is a gap untraversed, like the space between galaxies. Every John Hughes high school movie cliché is true.

Charlotte didn't look up, but you spotted her unclipping her nametag. She doesn't want company. Near miss. You almost walked right up to her to say something friendly and cool. You change course for the lunch counter when it occurs to you that "say something cool" isn't nearly specific enough. What would you say?

Nobody's behind the counter, so you pretend to look out the same front window Charlotte's gazing through. Her hairstyle hasn't changed since high school, but why mess with perfection? An outsider might think she needs a style update. To you? It's like your high school fantasy girl has been waiting, unchanged. Sure, she's older, but her full red lips and high cheekbones look softened. Her face is kinder now that she isn't so lean from doing cartwheels and flips all day.

Someone moves behind the screen to the kitchen and you clear your throat as if you're a busy man with places to be and money to make. A big bald guy comes out. You recognize his face but the name doesn't come. He looks like a guy who looks old for this age, like he picked late fifties early on and decided to stick with that until he grew into it.

"Eggs over easy and a coffee."

He looks around you to look at Charlotte. You're not sure what his look means since he looks like he chose permanently irritated at the same time he picked out his age. "How about scrambled? Scrambled's better."

You don't want scrambled, but it's more important to look decisive instead of looking fussy. You tell the big ape yes.

"Leaded or unleaded?"

"Hm?"

"The coffee." He says it slow, like you're stupid to be confused, even for a moment.

"Unleaded," you say, "Uh, decaf, I mean."

He smiles. It's not a nice smile. "Sausage or bacon with your eggs?"

"Sausage?"

"Uh-huh. We're out of brown bread. White okay?"

"Toasted," you say.

"Have a seat, white bread."

He shuffles off, sniffing like he needs to blow his nose but can't be bothered. You turn around, hoping Charlotte will stare at you, eyes bright with recognition. You want to see that moment when her face changes and her smile warms and spreads. Instead, she's seems fixated on the highway traffic.

You hold your breath and wave to her as you slide into her booth. "Hey, I know you," you say. Of course you do. You lusted after her as soon as your hormones woke up. You wait for the moment of recognition, but it doesn't come. Her face is frozen in concern and you're just some asshole stranger invading her space, presuming. You should have kept standing and introduced yourself before barreling in. Now you're already in the booth and you can't give up ground.

"Jimmy. Jimmy Pullnitz," you say. Why didn't you just say, "James, from high school"?

"Ah," she says.

What the fuck does 'ah' mean?

"It's good to see you again, Charlotte."

"You, too," she says. And she smiles.

Inside you chest, something breaks. You've been back home for weeks, hoping to run into her. You've driven by Merry's, looking in, waiting to chill enough so you could look casual when you appeared. You hadn't managed that, of course. Instead, you put your best suit on. Mom asked you where you were going "all gussied up".

"Out," you said. For Charlotte, you're ready with an explanation: you're just visiting, fresh from a business trip. You didn't want to show up looking to Charlotte like a local wearing a red plaid shirt and a Kenworth hat or a Dawgs jersey.

Jerseys.... She's asking you where you live. "At home, with my mother now." No, that's not a good answer. So you say Jersey. You should have said New York.

Wait, what? Did she say she'd been traveling? Mom told you "That Charlie girl" worked at Merry's and lives in an apartment over Molton's hardware.

Why is she saying she's headed to New York? There's a gap in the conversation so you say something tired about the weather. You say something about Mom's lungs and the humidity. Oh. So. Stupid. So banal. James Bond would handle this reunion much better.

You wish you hadn't lost the South Carolina job. You wish you'd couch-surfed with friends until a job popped up. But a man needs a lot of friends and a lot of different couches so he doesn't wear out his welcome.

You're so buried in lies by now that you tell the truth just to even things up a little. You don't want to be back in the hometown you hated. You told Mom your life would start when you headed off to college. You were so hateful to her when you were a teenager. Now that she's losing her marbles, you want to take all that back. Even though the stuff about escaping to freedom in the city was true.

You tell Charlotte you thought about being a teacher. School was so good. You hardly cracked a book and, with all those good grades, no one suspected how lazy you are.

You're talking to Charlotte. That hair. Those eyes. That full-lipped, lying mouth of hers is telling you about how she's working in New York. You want to tell her it's okay. She, of all people, doesn't have to put on airs. In that time before you escaped, when everybody called you Jimmy even though you hated it? You barely knew Charlotte, but she was the one good thing about high school.

You look at her. And look. And yearn. As much as you want to tell her you know she's lying, you don't. She looks happy. She doesn't deserve to be slapped with the truth. Not after all she's done for you. And who are you to call her on her shit? You're broke down on the road of broken dreams yourself.

Somehow this conversation has devolved. The Goddess Cheerleader Waitress and the Unemployed Nerd: tired is the word. You're ready to thank her for her time. You'll move to another booth — no, you'll ask for breakfast to go. You'll find a bench by the old tennis courts and eat cold eggs alone. That way Charlotte won't be embarrassed.

You had it in your head that this would go a different way and you'd act differently. You can't remember why you thought that.

"Charlie," you interrupt her from her babbling. You're just about to slide out, stand up and escape. If you stay, you'll embarrass her and that would embarrass you. You've got to get out of town. You don't want to run into Charlotte in town after this. There's only one supermarket, so you'd run into her eventually and what would either of you say then?

Your older brother will lend you some money. You'll head north and start to work on making some of the lies you told Charlotte true. Your older sister will have to look in on Mom. Mom's still got it together just enough. The family needs you to make money more than they need you to move into your mother's basement.

It's at that moment, just when you're about to say goodbye to Charlotte, that the big ape in back sneezes hugely and the snot hits the grill. You almost throw up. Charlotte is laughing at you. You're just about to call her a bitch between dry heaves when she grabs your hand and pulls you toward the door.

Her hand is soft and smooth and strong, tiny in your palm. The door slams behind you and she calls you James.

What the Booth Thought

These two lying sad sacks come in here and rub their assholes all over my face. They both need to move out and move on, for Christ's sake.

Prep vs. Perp

Tucker forgot to flush the history. You warned him about porn on the computer. When you take the Mac away, he'll text his friends on the iPod you gave him for Christmas. The iPod will have to go into your gun safe, too.

Disappointed, you lift the mattress. Nothing there. That's where you kept all your pornographic magazines when you were his age, but magazines are passé now.

Time's gone so fast. It wasn't that long ago your dad told you to get his belt. You promised yourself when Tucker was born that you'd never be that dad. You'd never tell your kid to go get your belt. Now you worry you've been too soft on your son. You worry he'll be too fragile to meet the challenges of such a hard world.

The bottom of his closet is a mess, but you don't find any contraband. How can he stand to live this way? There is no order to his room. How can he find anything? You'll add a weekend of cleaning this pigsty to his punishment. He'll cooperate with that plan or you'll dig the snow shovel out of the shed. Anything left on the floor will be gone. You'll just shovel it all into garbage bags and take it to Goodwill. He'll just have to wear whatever's left.

You don't want to be a hard ass, but Tucker's had it too easy. You're afraid he'll grow up to be a loser. He's not into competitive sports and that's a bad sign. Barbara said to let him alone and now, just as you predicted, he's spoiled. How will he cope? How will he live? The world is going to chew him up and shit him out.

You look through the papers on his desk. No love letters to, or from, any girls. If you were his age, the way girls are today, you like to think you'd tear it up. You find no love letters to, or from, any boys, either. Good. You don't know how you'd deal with that and Tucker's got enough problems.

His grades are okay — better than yours ever were, that's for sure. But smart as he is, his grades could be better. He's got his mother's brains, but he doesn't have your guts. He doesn't have a head for money and he's a quart low on ambition.

The thing that bothers you most is, Tucker could be a wheel. He's a sunny kid. People like him. He makes friends easily, like picking up quarters. But he's too nice. The world will destroy your son and then he won't be a sunny kid anymore and that will be your fault. You are failing to prepare him. What will you do?

His shirt drawer is stiff in its slot. At first you think it's just off its track. When you take out the drawer, you find the envelopes duct taped to the underside. The manila envelopes are so thick they rubbed against the pants in the drawer below.

You take a deep breath. Is that...? You know that smell. Your head gets hot while cold dread pools in your belly. Your hands tremble. The first envelope is filled with buds and rolling papers.

You sit on his bed listening to your heart pound. Barbara will be home in an hour. What will you do if Tucker comes home early from senior boys' basketball practice? Do you keep silent until you and Tucker and Barbara can sit around the dining room table and hash it out? This isn't about failing to do chores around the house or teenage attitude. One family meeting won't fix this.

Should you go get Tucker, yank him from the gym in front of all his friends? Should you haul him home and tell him, "Go get my belt"? Call the police and derail the failure train right here and now in one massive crash that will take years to recover from?

Is it already too late for that? Do you even have it in you to do that? You swore you wouldn't become your father, and here you are, going through your only son's room. If you hadn't come in here snooping, you wouldn't have to deal with this now. Now that you've started, you can't stop.

You look at the buds a long time. You've heard marijuana is stronger than in your day. To get a buzz, it takes a lot less than it used to. You feel the other envelope, worrying it will be full of harder drugs. It's thick and sort of familiar, too. If it's sheets of acid, Tucker's doomed.

How are you ever going to afford to send him to rehab on what you make? Does the company cover any of the bills for recovery from drug abuse? Even if they do, Marge in the front office is a blabbermouth. Everyone in the company will know. They're still talking about the senior vice president's prostate operation, idly speculating on whether he can still get it up for his trophy wife. Marge will flap her lips and you — father of the drug addict — will never get a promotion from your lousy job into a slightly less lousy job.

You feel your jaw tighten and you open the second envelope. It's the last thing you expected from Tucker. The tens, twenties and fifties are neatly wrapped with thick, flat elastic bands. You count the money. This is more than you could gross in commissions in half a year. Tucker is fucking loaded.

You sit on the bed for a long time, counting the money again and again. A tear rolls down your cheek and hangs on your chin until you finally wipe it away with the back of your hand. You aren't thinking of the cost of rehab anymore. The danger of the police savagely beating your son senseless isn't what's making you cry for the first time since your dad died.

What's on your mind is how your father would have handled this. He'd barrel around the house, chasing you and screaming. Something ceramic or glass would be broken. Whenever you think of your father, you picture him just like that: always worried about you, always in a rage. He loved you so much, but the deepest memories you have are about the time he sold your dog because you forgot to walk him. He put his fist through your bedroom wall because you wouldn't stop crying.

At your father's funeral you cried, not from grief, but because you felt no grief at all. Today you cry not for your spoiled, soft, drug dealer son, but for the fact that you don't know Tucker any better than your dad knew you.

Tucker will be home soon. You put the money back in the envelope. You put fresh tape on the bottom of the drawer so it moves in and out without sticking. You take out just enough buds for one blunt. You go out on the patio, fire up the barbeque and light the smoke off the hot grill. You'll boil some corncobs tonight and surprise everyone with pork chops, even though this isn't pork chop night.

The world will not eat up your boy. After dinner, you'll sit with Tucker and talk about what college he will attend next year. He can afford a better school than you thought. He can afford a better school than you could ever send him to.

The weed makes you cough a little. You remember this taste. You remember this feeling: despite everything that's wrong, things are going to be right.

Musclehead

You think mean is cool? Nah. Mean is mean. People don't respect you. That's fear. You keep showing everybody how big your muscles are. You keep showing off how dangerous you are. But all I hear is, "Love me, love me, love me!"

But they won't love you. Not until you pull that air hose out of your ass and deflate that deceiving ego by about 500 p.s.i.

Dick!

The Revolution Will be Televised

When the revolution comes, you will not be out front of a mob chucking Molotov cocktails at police carrying bloody riot shields.

When the revolution comes, you will not be safe in a bunker with years of freeze-dried food on infinite shelves, safe from civil disintegration and zombie attack.

When the revolution comes, you will be in the same spot you've been for all the other cataclysms: the San Francisco monster quake; the Santa Monica wildfires; Katrina; mile-wide tornadoes; multiple assassination attempts; Iraq Wars I and II; 9/11; Sarah Palin's run at the vice -presidency; and Michael Jackson's funeral. For all of them, you were in front of your television.

The Revolution will be televised. You'll be able to record it when the banks fall (figuratively) and then you'll be able to watch it when the banks collapse (literally) into burning rubble surrounded by chanting mobs (torches and useless ATM cards in their raised, clenched fists.)

If you don't start that day baked, you will certainly end it that way. Save some of your stash for medicine to hide from the Mad Max marauders.

When the revolution comes, anybody who talks to you will demand something from you. Or they'll say, over and over, "It's happened over and over for centuries, but I never thought it could happen to us."

Legacy

Your dad always got up early and never came downstairs without first shaving. Shoes shined, eager to start the day — that kind of guy. The guy he was when he left for work got beat down and shaped the man he was when he returned home. The guy who came home at the end of the day was angry, not eager.

"I feel whipped. I feel like a beat dog," Dad said. That customer said this. This customer said that.

Before supper was laid out before him, he would stalk back and forth. "I need a drink," he'd say. "Pour me a stiff one." He'd run through the day's atrocities, repeating the same story again and again, then relating it to other, similar stories. But they were all the same story: Retail made him somebody's bitch.

When you were close to graduating from high school he told you to get a degree in business. Why? He didn't say it was so you could be just like him and join the family business. He didn't say it, but you knew. When you were a little kid, he wanted you to copy his haircut, too.

So you refused to shave. You didn't go to business school. You ran away from everything he was.

꠸

Now your dad's retired, arthritic but free. You will never retire because you were too good to eat shit in a retail job every day. While you're smoking weed in the middle of the day and worrying about your bills, Dad's hobbling around Floridian beaches. He says he's happy. You suspect he's not really happy, just tough.

Through the clouds you go deep. You look backwards and forwards through time and you see how every choice you made led you down this path. Every time you choose, there are fewer choices ahead (which made you afraid to make too many choices.) Your life is an upside down pyramid; sluice gates out to sea; wide to narrow; the all to the nothing.

Sure, you're poor and chained to dead end jobs. As long as you stay high and keep making jokes, you can still say you rarely eat shit.

But make no mistake. By most people's measure? Your dad won.

What You Will Remember

No matter how many houses are destroyed, the rising and falling howl of sirens goes on through the night. Your dad says those are civil defense alarms, from way back when the worry was nuclear missiles. "Plague and mushroom clouds were the only worry," he says.

You nod. "Mushrooms taste bad."

He smiles. He hasn't done that for a long time. "When those civil defense sirens were put up, nobody paid attention to the clouds at all," he says. "The weather, I mean."

Since The Cull, the grown-ups say there are only two jobs left: roofers and funeral directors. When there's a break in storm fronts, the Electric Men come out to coat the rooftops and the roads with white paint. The Electric Men only look like men from a distance. Up close they look like a column of boxes with long spidery legs to climb over fallen trees.

The paint is like a big flat battery and the white paint is supposed to cool the atmosphere. "Between the winds and the paint, the bots will keep going long after...." Dad doesn't finish.

Nurses and doctors still have jobs, but Mom says they don't have the time or tools they used to have. "There's no medicine for fancy problems." The sisters' eyes will stay white, for instance.

The two old women, Eugenia and Euphoria are twins. They look like a pair of witches from your old picture books. The sisters are nice, though. A long time ago when the sisters were the family maids and dad was a little boy, your father almost drowned in a pool. The sisters jumped in together to save him even though they could hardly swim. When Dad told you that story, you went to each of the old ladies, hugged them, and told them they were good witches. Eugenia and Euphoria laughed a long time.

Eugenia, the sister who speaks, often says she's the good witch. Euphoria's memory isn't very good. "We don't have two sets of memory. We're the same person times two, so I keep track of things for Euphoria."

The sirens are wailing again, rising and falling, rising and falling. The sisters cover their ears and squooch up their faces, but to you, the sirens are exciting. You go to the window and search the dark for funnel clouds. Jagged lightning stretches across the sky, freezing everything for a moment in white flashes. You've never seen a freight train, but you've been told over and over that the wind makes that same loud, rumbly sound.

You close your eyes and watch the white flashes through your eyelids. It goes on and on. Thunder drowns out the sirens. You'd stay at the window, watching and waiting for the funnels. People do. Mom calls it the suicide trance. The tornadoes travel in packs. They lift trees and swirl them around and around like a poorly mixed drink in a tall glass, if the glass was miles wide and reached up to space.

Dad pulls you away from the window roughly by an elbow and hurries you downstairs. The house is mostly untouched, though a couple of months ago one of the greenhouses was destroyed. Mom stepped in some shattered glass in the yard and now her foot hurts all the time.

Before you were born, the family used to go to the cellar. When Mom was still fat with you in her belly, Dad had another building made. He calls it the back building, but most of it is underground. On top, it looks like a small garden shed. Underneath, the walls are cool and gray and there are no pictures. You call it your fort.

You don't mind the fort as much as the grown-ups. Their legs are too long. You'd rather watch the lightning, but you can see faces in the walls if you squint and stare. The patterns in the gray rivers of cracks and leaked water make strange, long faces that yawn and cry and need. The faces in the walls look like they're trying to say something you can't hear.

The fort does have much more room in it than it used to, so now you can swing your yo-yo around and make mistakes without hitting a box or a grown-up.

"Spacious," Mom says to Dad, frowning.

You like it. You can spread out the sketchbooks Dad gave you to draw and color. The boxes of freeze-dried food smelled of plastic and the musty cardboard made you sneeze. When the boxes pressed you too close to the wall, you couldn't see the concrete faces.

The ground above the fort shakes. "Megastorm," Mom whispers over and over and lays on the floor trying to get comfortable. She says the cold feels good on her back. "The air feels too close," she says.

Close air, you know, is the water in the air you can't see. Dad says "humidity" but Mom says stuff like "close." She talks like that sometimes, like it's still the time before. She called you

"Shug" for a long time before Eugenia explained it was short for "sugar."

"What's sugar?" you asked.

Mom props her hurt foot up on the lower bunk. You love climbing the little ladder into the top bunk bed. Up there, with your nose close to the ceiling, you feel closer to the power of the storms.

Dad pours a cup of rainwater into a bag. It pops and sizzles. You always ask if it's going to be peach cobbler (your last birthday present) and dad always shakes his head.

"When I asked my father what was for dinner," Dad says, "it was always the same thing on the menu: Shut up and eat."

The sisters laugh politely. No one has any new stories. Hiding from tornadoes for days at a time, you've heard all their stories: how dad met mom; about what riding horses was like: how there used to be so many people they were born in hospitals and now there aren't so many babies anymore.

Sometimes you get so tired of old people's stories you go sit on the toilet just to get away from them. You come out when you can't stand the smell. It's not the poop smell that makes you wrinkle your nose and breathe through your mouth; it's the stink of the chemicals that eat the poop.

You don't want to leave the faces in the wall — if you squint just so, they move a little — so tonight you don't hide in the toilet. Instead, you sigh and say, "Old stories are for old people."

You don't realize you've even said it out loud, or that you shouldn't have said it, until everyone gets quiet.

After a time, Dad says that out in the world there are men and women who work day and night, very hard. They work in deserts, turning all the sand into glass. "Geo-engineering will make way for new stories, sweetheart."

You've heard the word. Geo-engineering means making mirrors. The people in the desert will build so many mirrors that some of the sun's heat will be reflected back into space.

"The oceans will evaporate less and the thermals will ease," Dad says. "They just have to figure out how to get the mirrors into space. It's tricky because there are fewer people and fuels to help make it happen."

You ask how they'll get all those mirrors into space without breaking them. "If you break a mirror, that's seven years bad luck, right?"

"Rotten luck," Dad says.

You're seven. Somebody must have broken a lot of mirrors already for the world to be as scary and hot and wet as it is.

"They're working on it, Shug," Mom says from the floor. She sounds very tired.

The people in the desert used to use rockets, but there's only so much fuel and the fire and smoke from all the rockets helped make the weather worse. Dad says they're working on an elevator that goes all the way to space. "Imagine that! One long rope that stretches up into orbit."

It's dark in the fort — just one crank lantern — but you spot a tear sliding down Mom's cheek. One of the sisters — you're not sure but you think it's Euphoria — scuttles over and awkwardly lowers herself to the floor until she's cross-legged. The old woman lifts your mother's head into her lap and strokes her long hair.

Dad hands you the sizzling bag. "Spaghetti."

You make a face but you don't complain. You used to complain when you were little but you're a big girl now. You used to whine about what there was to eat, but you stopped because Mom wouldn't stop crying.

"We're all soldiers with duties now," Dad says. "Your duty is to be a big girl."

You don't want to be a big girl.

After you eat, you go to the toilet. You take your time and enjoy the quiet. When the storms come, all the grown-ups seem to need to talk more. They think they're doing it for you, "distracting the kid."

When you come around the corner, you hear Eugenia whispering, "Eat Euphoria first. She's fatter."

That's distracting.

Euphoria rarely speaks but she says back, loudly, "You're fatter around the mouth, you old bitch!" Dad laughs along with the twins. Then they join Mom in her silence and the thunder sounds closer now: rolling in, banging on, crashing down, crashing in.

You wait a long time for sleep and when it finally comes, it feels like a slow blink. Dad tells you the storm front is moving west to do battle with the mountains.

It is good to get outside. After the rains, the air smells fresh and cooler, like it's been scrubbed of dirty things. You can't see it in the air, but you can feel a difference. The breeze makes the air light, just as Mom's pain makes the air in the concrete shelter heavy. The long grasses, sweet enough to eat, whisper something you can't quite hear.

Dad takes your hand and surprises you by taking you with him to the greenhouse. "Let's survey the damage. Whenever a storm comes through, soldiers have to survey the damage and make repairs to be sure things last."

Dad says it's midday, but the daylight is a strange yellow-green gloom. Some tree limbs are down around the tennis courts. You've never played tennis. It's too dangerous to play at night or during storm attacks and it's too hot during the day.

The fallen branches are not from nearby trees, but dropped by the wind on its way elsewhere to the purple mountains.

You tell Dad you hope everyone in the mountains is safe in their forts, too.

"Not everyone — " He stops, takes a deep breath and pulls you toward the greenhouse. "We could gather up those branches. I've read that some barks make a nice tea."

"Ew."

"No, really! And birch! I think it's birch that has medicine in it."

"Would the medicine make Mom better?"

He shrugs. "It might help Mom. Or make good paper...if you run out of paper."

As you pick your way across the tennis courts Dad tells you about bugs. "Packed with protein, they are."

"I'm not eating any bugs."

"You used to, sometimes, when you were little. It was always in breakfast cereal."

"Big girls don't eat bugs."

"Hungry girls and smart soldiers do. Lots of protein."

You change the subject. "Mom used to be really good at tennis."

He doesn't say anything, so you ask him if you can go to the desert and make mirrors.

"I think there are more deserts than there used to be, so maybe someday, honey."

"Mom doesn't think the mirrors will work." You don't say it like a question so he doesn't exactly disagree with you.

"Mom doesn't. I do."

"Why do you think it'll work?"

"Just because it has to."

"Why?"

"There are a lot fewer people now."

"Where'd they all go?"

He gives you a hard look, like you did something wrong. "They are where they always were. Dreamland."

"Where?"

Dad looks away. "I mean they aren't in Kansas anymore." The way he sounds, you don't want to ask any more questions.

There are tomatoes in the greenhouse. Dad tells you they're good for your prostate and laughs. His laugh sounds the way the toothy edge of a hunting knife looks.

Dad picks some weeds and tucks them into the leather bag at his hip. "Our best crop," he says. "Grows anywhere. Good medicine."

"Will it fix Mom's foot?"

"It fixes everything, but just for a little while."

"How's it taste?" you ask.

"Like skunk's butt," he says. You go into a giggle fit and fart and your father finally lets out a laugh that sounds right. You have no way of knowing it, but you do know. That big laugh comes from The Time Before.

Someday when you're an old soldier, you'll tell stories around a campfire. You'll tell this story to the young ones. You won't remember the explosive thunder, the ripping winds or the pretty arcs of chain and ball lightning.

Incredibly, you will have long forgotten the yearning, desperate faces of the ghosts you saw in the walls. They reached for you, needing to tell their stories. Their faces said they were lonely. They wanted you to join them. When you get old, there will be no walls and you won't think about the souls trapped in walls anymore. Time and the wind wipes takes away all the debris.

Instead, you'll remember your father's laugh.

Body of Work

You step out of the punishing sun into a dark room. You've driven for hours today, five on pavement, two on dirt. Sunblind, yellow and green spots obscure the room so all you see is dark shapes. It seems to be a surprisingly large one-room shack. There's the shape of a slight woman against the back wall sitting by a pot-bellied stove.

"You're Joe's friend," she says with a voice like milk. It's not a question.

"He sent me," you say, unsure of what to say or do.

She moves toward you through the gloom and, in a sliver of light from the crack of the door, you see she's not a young Latina, but neither is she old. Her long hair is streaked with silver and pulled back in a girlish ponytail to show off her high cheekbones, full lips and large, heavy-lidded eyes. She doesn't even come up to your shoulder.

"D'jou bring da money?"

If Joe hadn't told you she was blind, you'd think she was a mean bitch with that flat stare. You hold out the thick envelope and it takes you a moment before you get that she doesn't see what you're doing. You flick the envelope with the back of your hand and say, "American dollars."

She puts out her hand and you place the packet in her palm. "Good," she says. "How is my friend, Joseph?"

"Pushy." He sent you out to the middle of nowhere. If not for the GPS in the Jeep, you'd never have found this place.

The woman shrugs and moves back to the kitchen area, rippling the bills in the envelope.

It only occurs to you now that you could have given her a stack of singles and she wouldn't know the difference until you were safely back across the border. You dismiss the thought: too much of a risk. It doesn't pay to fuck around in foreign countries. All the way here you were sure some crazy gang would run you off the road and play a game of decapitate the gringo for his Jeep. They do that around here. The stories are crazier than anything that ever came out of the Los Angeles gang wars.

"Wash up out back," she says. "Get the road dust off you. There's a pump hooked up to a hose from the wall out back. When you come back in, be naked."

You don't move. You hate indecision, but Joe didn't say anything about getting naked. In fact, all he said was, "You need to go see the blind woman." He handed you the envelope full of money and programmed your GPS and said you weren't allowed back in his compound until "you got your head on straight."

So it was exile or be naked somewhere in Mexico. If you're going to have sex with this blind whore, you don't need to go get washed up. Whores don't get to complain about a little road dust.

"Go," she says. "Don't worry. There's nobody around for miles and sure won't be able to see your bits and pieces. We are all born naked."

You laugh. "You ever been to England? 'Bits and pieces' sounds — "

"Yeah." She slips into a formal British accent that sounds right off the BBC: "A few years at Oxford. You're stalling, chickenshit. Do hose off."

So you go out back. There are a couple of goats, but that's all, so you strip down and fold your clothes into a neat pile by your cowboy boots.

The water is cool, but in this heat, the well water is fresh and relieving. The goats come close, looking for water. Their horns are at crotch height and their marble eyes make you nervous, so you cover your balls with one hand and scoot away to get back into your boots.

You're halfway back to the front door before you realize you don't have a towel, so you run your hands over your body, squeegeeing water droplets. You shake your long hair and ring it out.

Walking around outside naked feels strangely liberating and uncomfortable at the same time. You're a ridiculous rangy cowboy, wearing only your boots and carrying your billfold and passport. Did Joe set you up, sending you out here? You wouldn't mind banging the whore, but Joe's not the kind of guy to give you that sort of present.

Why send you this far to get laid when there's no shortage of skanks on your own block? And how would getting screwed out here in Nowhere, Mexico screw your head on straight? Did the bitch have magic pussy? What kind of prostitute goes to Oxford but ends up blind out here between rattlesnakes and tumbleweeds?

She's changed from a skirt into shorts and she's now wearing a t-shirt that says, "Garmy Strong!", whatever that means. As soon as she hears your step, she tells you to lose the boots at the door. You're glad she's blind. All this uncertainty makes your crotch lizard feel small.

"First, drink the tea," she says. She holds out a Tim Horton's coffee mug.

"You get that in Canada?"

"Yes," she says, but pronounces it *jess*. You love that smooth voice. You wish she was more chatty just so you could hear her lips forms words. That accent must have driven all those British schoolboys nuts.

You sip the tea and almost spit it out. Instead, you wince. "Needs sugar," is all you say. No way you're going to look weak, even in front of someone who can't see you.

She shakes her head and jabs her chin up.

You drink the rest. Staring at her chest helps you to force the bitter liquid down. For such a small woman who's past the shiny side of forty? Fifty? She's not wearing a bra and her breasts are buoyant.

"Drink it quickly," she says. "There's a lot of work to do."

"Sounds kinda impatient for pillow talk."

She's doesn't smile.

When you've drained the last of the tea, she snatches the mug from your hand unerringly, as if she can see you just fine.

The blind woman gestures for you to follow her and you guess there's a bedroom in back. Instead she pulls back a ceiling-to-floor curtain to reveal a long padded table that stands about thigh high.

"Jesus! Joe sent me hundreds of miles into another fucking country to get a massage? I coulda just gone to the Valley and been home for dinner three days ago."

She looks pissed. "If Joseph sent you to me, you're not here for a happy ending."

She reaches into a tall jar three-quarters full of Planet Hollywood matchbooks. She lights a slender red candle at the head of the table. Once it's lit she walks around the table with it, lighting more tall, white candles.

"You gotta urinate first? This will take a while."

"Uh, no. Sweated it all out getting here."

She bends low to light more candles that form a large circle around the table. Some of the candles are Jesus candles, faces melted down evenly to short beards. There's also a Buddha candle, several squat honeycomb candles and a large purple candle that looks like a cherub holding a bunch of grapes on its shoulder.

As the light comes up in the room, you feel more naked. "That's a lot of candles, babe. You're not planning to barbecue me, are you?"

"Let's call that Plan B," she says. The voice is still smooth, but you can't detect any humor in it.

As you step closer, you notice the candle flames brighten. They turn red and blue. Then they flare high and stretch out to become flaming Stars of David. The angles in each flame get tighter and sparks, sharp as knives, begin to move through the air toward your face.

"Get on the table," she says. "Face down to start. You better hurry, gringo, before the world flips you over and rattles you around the room like you're a bug in a salt shaker."

Her hair has come loose and long tendrils shoot out, wrapping around your ankles and wrists. You try to speak, but your tongue is numb. You manage a moan, but that's all. You stumble onto the table and, with surprisingly strong hands, the little blind woman grabs your lower legs and yanks you the rest of the way into position. Instead of lowering your face to the oval pad, a black hole rushes up to meet you and sucks you in with irresistible gravity. The hole seems too small, like you're sucking air through a straw. You have to breathe fast so you can breathe at all.

"You will survive this," she says. Her voice seems to come from far away, maybe from deep space, and then echo all the way down to you at the bottom of a coal mine. "The question is not if you'll die," she adds. "The question is, how will you live afterward? You're going to see the truth of things. A guy like you...you see the truth, it's going to fuck you up, but in a good way."

"Who are you?" you say. You didn't care what her name was before. Now it seems very important that you know.

"Lena," she whispers, close to your ear.

Your mind empties. How much time has passed? Is this the part of Mexico where time doesn't apply at all? And what was in that tea?

As if she can hear your thoughts, Lena says, "The tea is the catalyst. The rest of the work you'll have to do on your own."

You feel the heat of her hands, an inch above the bare skin of your shoulders. Then she touches you very softly. The weight of her hands is no heavier than a spider's leg, but you feel an arc of electricity and see an arcing white light shoot into your heart.

And your heart begins to open.

You feel the warmth spread out, as if your body is thawing. You soften, and at first you think you can fight it, but the energy swallows you up and in your mind's eye you can see, hear, feel and taste all your cells powering up, lighting up. At your best, before the tea, your body might have felt like a live electrical wire. But this? Your heart is a nuclear core, running hot, melting through your defenses.

Your mind is a white light and the table is gone. You can still feel the pressure of the table's padding on your chest and face, but the candlelit floor is gone. Instead, you see a path. Part of you, far away, reassures you that what you are seeing is not real, but the voice sounds weak and unconvincing. You're leaving the known.

"Ahead of you is a path," Lena says, somehow seeing it, too. "Your choice. Will you follow where it goes?"

Your heart slams against your ribs. Stomach acid boils up to the back of your mouth. You choke it back, but regret it instantly. You should have thrown up and got the tea out of your system...or should you? You've been high before, lots of times, but never like this.

You say nothing but somehow Lena knows you are not following the path. She walks her fingers down your spine. Each pressure point turns you to butter...then you are water. Energy ripples out in circles from wherever she touches.

And you feel stronger, strong enough to step on the path.

Lena watches you from a corner of your childhood living room while your father beats you with a belt. Some older boys said terrible things about your older sister. You said nothing and when your sister told your father, he beat you mercilessly for not stepping up. He did you much more harm than anything the bullies would have done.

You're trying not to cry, refusing to succumb to your father's will. You didn't cry when your father beat you the first time. But now you look over and see Lena watching your struggle. Her eyes are large and soft and compassionate. Your dam breaks. Tears blur your vision.

The room swirls and now you are your father. And you are you. And you are a grown man, naked on a table, losing your mind somewhere in Mexico. You are chasing you into a kitchen. No, this is the kitchen in your childhood home in the mid to late '70s. You recognize the old Mix Master your mother used to mix the dough to make bread. The belt buckle whistles at your head in slow motion so you don't miss a detail. When the buckle strikes you in the right ear, it is agony.

You try to stop the hand that holds the belt, but you're not in control. You are just an observer feeling your father's rage. You watch your own humiliation. You hear your own cries.

And there's a fresh surprise: Under your father's anger, you feel his frustration and how afraid he is for your sister's safety. He's even scared for you. He knows he should not hurt you. Your father feels all these emotions at once. He is a ball of energy with no outlet but violence. His brain is supposed to be a sieve filtering out what he shouldn't do, but he's broken.

Lena's seeing eyes are filled with care and compassion. Her compassion reaches for you, touches you. Your heart opens a little more. For the first time, you feel compassion for your father.

The room swirls again and you are in a different kitchen. The Mix Master is gone. The toaster is modern. This was an old apartment from a string of shitty apartments. You're spanking your girlfriend's kid because he said you aren't his father. He says he doesn't have to listen to you.

You watch your red face and gritted teeth. You look like your dad. You hate yourself just as much as you hated him.

All that melts away and it's your first night in a federal prison. You're getting fucked from behind while three guys hold you down. The guy who's not fucking you — the guy who's smoking and watching and laughing? You hate him the most.

Then you're in another cell. Looks like Joliet. You're the one doing the fucking this time. You don't really want to do this. It's like you're eating when you're already plenty full. It's not about the sex. It's just that your crying victim looks vaguely like the guy who laughed at your humiliation, who smoked and watched you get ass raped. Your cellmate must be punished for his weakness.

But somehow you love him, too, because you dominate him. He will never be a threat to you. You will always hold this power over him. And you feel no fear.

And now you're the victim. You're getting fucked in the ass by yourself. To your horror, Lena is watching. Inside hell, the blind woman witnesses what you have done.

Lena's face is an impassive mask, but her hands shift to the dragon tattoo on your left bicep. The red dragon comes alive, shrieks, flaps leathery wings and sinks sharp bloody teeth into your neck. You'd scream if you could, but instead you're outside yourself looking down on the scene.

You've seen yourself from this third party perspective before, several times: when you went into shock as you fell down some stairs as a kid; when the cops beat you down bad after you got mouthy and drunk at a baseball game; the convenience store security cam video in court; those times you were in prison and things were done to you.

Lena frowns and moves to your feet, squeezing hard. You watch her nail beds go white as she closes her fingers around your soles. "Do not dissociate. Come back in your body. Stay with the scene of the crime."

You shoot back into your body and you feel all the pain at once. You feel the pain you inflicted and the pain inflicted upon you. You understand now that you gave worse than you got. You thought the world was shittier than you. The weight of being wrong is crushing. You want to cry out and this time you can let it out.

First, you scream.

Later, you cry like a baby.

And you remember what Lena said. You skipped over it before, but it seems more important now. "We are all born naked," she said.

A yellow mist made of triangles forms in front of you. As you begin to calm yourself, to slow your breathing, the scene takes shape, becomes cohesive, moving from 2D to 3D. It's the path again.

No one has to invite you to take the path this time. You don't know where the yellow path of sand leads, but it's good. It's leading you away from what you were.

You understand now that when the path first appeared, Lena was trying to spare you pain. The farther you go along this path, the better you feel. The walking gets easier as the path gets firm. The path widens and becomes a road and it turns a brighter yellow. Soon you are walking on gold brick. You remember the movie from your childhood.

Your mother and father sat on either side of you on the living room couch. Your older sister was upstairs asleep but your father said you could stay up to watch. You said the movie made a mistake because when Dorothy and Toto arrive in Oz, the film goes from black and white to color. Your parents laughed together and your father gently tousled your hair.

You feel the Yellow Brick Road under your feet. You turn to Lena. She is younger here. Her hair is in pigtails. She's wearing a blue dress and bright red ruby slippers.

Lena smiles. She can see you perfectly and she even likes what she sees.... No. Better. She *forgives* what she sees. If a mere human can forgive you, then God just has to, right?

"You know what you're here for, yes?" She still says yes like jess. You guess that back in the world Lena is standing beside your body, speaking to you down a long mind line from Nowhere, Mexico in a one-room shack that's big enough to hold worlds.

"I think I will know what I'm here for," you hear yourself say. "I just have to ask the right question and I believe the answer will come."

"So?" she says, idly twirling a pigtail.

"What have I come here to get?" And the answer comes immediately: you're here to get a brain, a heart and to discover true courage.

"How will you get these things?" Lena asks, reading your mind again.

"I don't have to go anywhere," you hear yourself say. "I can just choose them. The dream will be real."

Coming back into your body is a shock, like falling into a pool of water unprepared. But the pool of water is the same temperature as your body, like one of Joe's isolation tanks. The pool is your body.

It takes several minutes before you feel like you're all the way back. When you try to speak again, you find you have cotton mouth. It's a familiar feeling from other drugs you've taken. You've had cotton mouth from doing a long bender of shooters in Vegas and from too much weed. But whatever was in that tea went bigger and deeper than any psychedelic you've ever done.

Lena is ready with the Tim Horton's mug. You give her a nervous look, but this time it's not the tea. It's just water.

"How do you feel?" Back on this plane, she's blind again. Here she's just a small woman in late middle age, but you see how beautiful she is now. Lena is Nowhere's good witch.

"I'm...shaky," you say.

"As a newborn deer," she says. "What will you do now?"

"Think a while. I've been operating on instincts for a long time. Things were beaten out of me and beaten into me. It was bad training. I've been thinking tough was an important thing, a value. I thought being tough was bigger and better than good."

"Somebody who feels they need to be that tough must be afraid so much."

"Yeah," you say. "Made me a douchebag."

She shrugs. You wish she had disagreed with you, but that she doesn't? That makes her the tough one. Honesty is her good witch power.

You try to get up but your arms can only tremble.

"You need to sleep for a day," she says.

You nod.

"And then?"

You know what she's doing. She's cementing the connection between Nowhere and Oz, making sure you'll do, not just think. "I'll do the manly thing. I'll have a nap and get my clothes and climb back in my Jeep and cry all the way back to California."

"Good start," Lena says. "Let all that bad stuff out."

"Then I'll get my scarecrow, tin man and lion together and make 'em work. I've got a lot of people to say sorry to, starting with Joe."

You know you will never see Lena again, although in the years to come you will send several men and women to visit her.

You close your eyes and, in a moment, you feel the blanket cover your body. Lena's warm hands spread it over your back. Your mom did that when you were little, too. Your last words to Lena are, "Thank you, mother."

Many years in the future, you will lie on clean white sheets, dying in a welcome haze. These drugs won't be Lena's tea, but at the end of this trip, you will be back on the Yellow Brick Road, heading back to the place where we all meet.

Your daughters will lean close so they can hear you mumble your last words. With your last breath you will say, "Thank you, mother."

You will be mourned.

Later, as they walk down the hospital corridor with their arms around each other, leaning in, your daughters will argue gently. Your eldest daughter will say you were thanking their lovely mother, your wife. Your youngest will say you must have been talking about your own mother.

They both will believe you were born in a little town in Michigan, too, but accidents of geography don't matter. You were a tin man, a scarecrow and a lion. But then you became a husband, a father and a person instead of a slave. You found out, not too late, that we are born where we begin again.

Your birthplace was Nowhere.

Pep

If you are like me and have found yourself living in the middle of Nowhere, welcome. We are the dazed, the confused, the disenchanted and the inexplicably hopeful. We are ironic optimists and mean (but funny!) pessimists. And we are legion. You are not alone.

Everyone comes to Nowhere at some point in their lives: we live in a small Nowhere town with too-nosy neighbors. Or we are in a Nowhere city, disenfranchised and anonymous among strangers who don't care about us. Nowhere can be geographic or it can be your quarter-life crisis, your mid-life crisis, your job loss, your divorce, your fear for the future, your worry that life will change and the horror you feel when you're sure your life will not change. You are holding an antidote to being smack in the middle of Nowhere. It's a great place to start out from. When you start in Nowhere, you're like the fattest kid at fat camp: You've got a lot of potential.

"To realize your potential." You've heard that awful phrase when you were called to the principal's office and in vapid valedictorian speeches. "Realizing potential" is at once our greatest aspiration and a dreaded self-help cliché that's been beaten into a coma, strangled in the ICU, buried, dug up and beaten again.

Instead, work on being the best you. That's the only self-help you need, stoner or not.

Tough Guy

You've disappeared into a university, a city of students, goodwill hunting your education with just a library card and a smile, determined to write like Hemingway. You tell yourself that, someday, a generation of English majors will take your minimalism as homage instead of a rip off. When Hemingway comes back in style, you will be a non-ironic literary star. You will live free, a man conducting himself on his own terms. Your parents will be sorry.

Gay isn't just how you're born. Gay is the network you plug into. You don't just make friends. You remake friends into the family of your choosing. The exiled and disavowed and rejected determine their relations among themselves so that they, too, will have a home. Your people support brothers and sisters chosen by merit instead of by accidents of birth.

You knew your tribe was out here somewhere, waiting for you to join them. As soon as you were old enough, you began your hero's journey. You left Poeticule Bay to find your people and build your new family. (Straights wish they had a group half as tight, so breeders choose churches and volunteer fire departments and the Elk's Club for their support network.)

When you get to the city, you've got no money so you work the counter at QuickPickens. The stupid name suggests a store that sells donuts made of pork, but you really sell art supplies and graphics services. You steal paper from the photocopiers for your writing and sleep in the park, a knife in your hand under your pillow. Your backpack is your pillow.

Then the boss, George Pickens, decides he can trust you with a key to the shop. You can finally sleep indoors. George is impressed that you are never late. He thinks you are a model employee until he finds your sleeping bag behind the recycling bin in the back. He lets you keep your part-time job as long as you promise not to sleep in the store.

Finding a bed for the night is hit and miss. You start hiding in the school library. Not a few times, a security guard shakes you awake and you pretend you fell asleep studying. That way you are noble instead of a homeless bum.

It's a small liberal arts college. There are warm, narrow beds you can charm your way into. You even sleep with a few girls until you realize that the girls willing to sleep with you are just as willing to give you a place on the floor as long as you're entertaining. Entertaining is easy for you, especially when you let loose and be yourself.

Then it occurs to you to make a t-shirt at QuickPickens. All it says is, "Available." Up until then your flirting strategy is simply to ask a guy on campus if he is in the drama or the dance program. That t-shirt opens the door to the underground social network. Plus, you sell t-shirts under the table to all the gay guys so they can identify each other without tipping off townie gay bashers.

You have a little money, but you are still never sure if you have a bed for the night. You are getting too skinny, so you steal a cafeteria card from a date and put your picture on it.

You get to shower regularly after you repeat the trick with a university gym card.

When you aren't at QuickPickens, you're at the school library. Most of your dates never guess you aren't actually enrolled. Occasionally you sit in on a class, but you prefer books to people. Your only extravagance is calligraphic pens, ink refills and leather journals for your notes, outlines and stories. Someday, you're sure, these journals will form the basis of a retrospective on your brilliant career.

You're eighteen months into your freedom ride on the brightest day of the year. The sun is dazzling and you feel great. Then a large man with a granite face sits next to you on a bench outside the library. You lower your sunglasses and consider him, but he's too old and scary for you, bed or no bed.

"Your parents miss you, Benny," he says.

You say nothing and open your backpack. You're rereading Sartre's *The Stranger*. You slide your copy into your pack and stand to leave.

The big man reaches up and wraps a paw around your upper arm and squeezes hard, forcing you back into your seat. You grit your teeth and tell him to let go. He digs a thumb into your bare triceps and you almost scream.

"Listen, twink! I've traveled a lot of miles and done a lot of searching to find you. You're a long way from Poeticule Bay."

You bite your lip. It might bleed. "I'm not going back to Maine."

He digs his thumb deeper into the meat of your arm so he can tweak the bone and, despite yourself, you cry out.

"How did you find me?" you say.

"One of your boyfriends thinks you're a real bitch."

Dan. It has to be Dan. He wanted to get serious and you walked out. A week later you came back but asked for his couch for the night instead of his bed.

"You're coming with me. Your parents are waiting at a Chinese restaurant around the corner. You come with me easy, have a sit down and discuss your situation."

"I don't have a situation," you say. "Not anymore."

"Shut up."

"What if I just start screaming?"

"Then I'll break your fuckin arm. And I'll have a talk with the dean. I imagine the campus police will be embarrassed that you've been mooching off the school. They'll have your picture up everywhere. You won't ever eat or sleep here again."

"Don't do that. I've already been thrown out of one home. This is my home now. I'm making a life here."

"Oh, please," he says. "Don't be so dramatic. You weren't exiled. You're just another fruity runaway, running from the people who know you best. When the people who know you well all think you suck, guess what? That's on you."

"I'm not going anywhere with you."

He sighed heavily. "You parents hired me to get you and I'm not cheap, so I guess they care."

"No, they don't. I embarrass them and all they're worried about is what the neighbors think. That's not love."

"You put your parents through hell."

"They put me through hell first."

"Not interested, boy. Come with me." He digs his thumb in deeper still, separating muscle and bone.

You shriek but he keeps it up, unconcerned who might see. People slow down, heads turn, but everyone keeps walking. No one wants to get involved. No one knows you well enough to care. He is so sure no one will object, your rage rises to match the pain. But pain is too small a word for what you're feeling.

"I'm an adult," you say. "You make me come with you, it's kidnapping."

The big man smiles for the first time. A gold tooth glints in his cruel mouth. "You stole money from your father. Suppose they press charges? Any idea what happens to a little boy like you in jail? You cellmate will punch your teeth out first, just for easy access." He looks you up and down. "Or maybe you'd like that?"

He begins to drag you away. His eyebrows shoot up in surprise. He looks down. The blade is buried between his ribs to the pearl-handled hilt. He sits on the bench again, his stare never leaving the knife.

You snatch up your pack, but before you disappear you look back. The red splotch on his side spreads. The man looks smaller.

"Don't just pull the blade out. You might live if you sit very still and wait for an ambulance. I'll call for one right away." And you do. The 911 operator wants to keep you talking. You tell the operator to tell your parents to stop looking for you.

The police will watch the trains and buses so you steal Dan's car and head north. You already have new ID ready. In fact, you have a small stack of cards with lots of different names. You didn't work at QuickPickens for the wage slavery.

You're tougher and smarter than they know. They thought you were a wimp. They called you fairy, fag, queer, homo. They think they know you. They fuckin don't. You endured high school in Poeticule Bay, Maine for years. That took more guts than the month or two it took the Marine Corps to make Dad a man. He thinks he had it tough as a soldier? Bullshit.

At least his war ended and he got to come home. You've still got enemies everywhere. Friends can betray you. Homophobes want to beat you and kill you. Most of the world is your enemy. Your family thinks they own you. They think they can pray the gay away.

They do not understand that you are a spy who never knows whom to trust. You have to be a warrior just to be what most people take for granted: left alone. And you are a motherfucking Viking. You're the man wending up the west coast in a stolen car after stabbing a bad guy. You wonder if the bad guy lived, but you don't wonder very long. Fuck 'em. To fight the power, you have to feel your power. They have no idea how scary you're prepared to be so you can stay free.

You smoke a jay and feel your shoulders loosen. What little American university town is small enough, tucked away, yet big enough to find your people? You have allies to find, a tribe to build, a family to remake.

Yes, your cheeks are wet, but there's a powerful rising through your chest, like you just might fly. That's what freedom feels like.

You press the accelerator.

Penny for Your Thoughts

You don't smoke but you slap on three nicotine patches, go to bed, and wait. When sleep swallows you, the show begins.

When you wake up in a hospital bed, the lights are blinking in and out. All the nurses are tall, beautiful women dressed in powder blue. They are all in white face — not like mimes or minstrels, but like David Bowie's makeup from his Ziggy Stardust days. They are striking, sparkly and a little alien.

When one of the nurses leans close, you notice she wears a line of black skull and bones pins down her cap. The cap looks like those flight attendants wore a long time ago when they were called stewardesses. "Doctor," she says, "you're needed in the O.R., stat, code blue, olly olly oxen free!"

Before you know it, gore soaks your sleeves. You're up to your elbows in guts, wielding a scalpel. You cut everything out. You're not in surgery to save any organs. All you see is the surgical field. The rest of the patient is covered in sterile sheets. That's why you're doubly surprised when the person you've hollowed out shudders on the operating table and raises its great spiny head.

The face has tiny, weak eyes and horny spikes on its forehead. Through thick ivory tusks, the dinosaur creature speaks to you in a decidedly gay German accent: "How does it go, dahlink? I vas sinking ve could go have a tea aftervard unt share our stories."

You begin to suspect something's amiss.

You stand back and look down. Your feet are bare. You're standing in fine, warm sand. A tall, stinking pile of pink and gray dinosaur guts steams beside you. You look up at the sun. It's slowly blinking in and out, there and not there. The sight is unnerving. You wonder why you aren't flying off into space every time the sun's gravity is negated.

"This," you conclude, "is ridiculous!"

A buxom nurse with bowling ball tits hanging out of the front of her uniform steps toward you. She holds out an ornately garnished glass on a silver tray. "Pina colada, Herr doctor?" she breathes, but hers is not a woman's voice. She speaks with the same fey dinosaur voice. Nonetheless, you want to feel the weight of those big tits in your palms.

When you reach out for the drink, you stumble forward and to stop from falling you make a grab for a breast. The nurse effortlessly encircles your wrist with her long spiny dinosaur tail. You hadn't yet seen that. She twists her tail and you're driven to your knees. You look up into her perfect marble face and scream in pain.

"You should aspire, dahlink," the nurse says. "If you are going to dream ziss hard, why not go flying around zee planet, or zee universe? You could be exploring, learning zee secrets of zee universe. Zere eze zo much to discover, ja? Sink of all you could learn about yourself!"

You wake up screaming when your wrist bangs against the clock on your night table. You knock the clock to the floor. Your head squeezes and your pulse races, pounding in your ears. You sit up cautiously, afraid of what you'll see, and search the room for Amazon nurses and dinosaurs in disguise.

Yes, you're sure now that you are back in your room. The slow blink of the neon motel sign across the street flashes red across your ceiling. Every night that shitty motel's sign goes on and off, on and off, on and off through the night. You wish you had enough money to buy up all its rooms so for just one night you could sleep in your own bed unharrassed without that red flash invading your nicotine dreams. The motel is so rife with bed bugs that the vacancy sign never gets a rest. And so, neither do you.

You grope for your glasses and try to focus on the digital clock upside down on the floor. The red numerals flash: 12:00, 12:00, 12:00.

You won't be able to sleep now so you get up and scrub your face hard with your knuckles. You might as well get up. There's an all-night coffee house down the street so you pull on some clothes. You're out of clean socks so you shove your bare feet into ratty old sneakers.

Though nicotine must still be in your system, you feel foggy. Espresso is the answer. Tonight's lack of decent sleep is really going to give tomorrow a lubeless ass fuck. Tim, the middle manager with too many teeth, will buzz like a mosquito in your ear. He whizzes by your cubicle every time he goes for a whiz and says every time, "Just checking in!" As if constant interruptions are a key component that helps you get his Power Point slides made.

On the plus side, you're pretty sure Tim is going to the bathroom so much he must have diabetes or a urinary tract infection. Maybe you'll luck out and Tim has bladder cancer. Or he could die in a happy, fiery plane crash on his next exotic business trip.

The coffee house is empty when you push through the door. No students or sad, aspiring screenwriters and failed novelists are slowly getting tans and skin cancer from screen radiation. You head to the counter, scanning for staff but no one's out front. However, someone's banging around in the back so you sit in the empty café and wait for the all-night barista.

There's no clock.

The café is like a casino in that way. The owners don't want you to have a sense of time under the constant white glow of fluorescent light. They want you to guzzle coffee until your stomach turns sour and pay for your wifi and never notice your life is slipping away. You get to leave when your money's gone. Or when you realize your novel will never get an agent no matter how many times you rework that query letter.

Book publishing has collapsed in on itself, sucked down the same black hole as music and movie stores. You've had a novel in a bottom drawer at work and slaved over it during your lunch hours while the rest of the staff go out in the sunshine. You felt pretty good about it.

Then Tim found it.

He read it aloud in front of everyone at the Monday morning sales meeting. Your vision flashed red in time with your throbbing headache. Tim mocked you with your pivotal, sensitive scene in which a teenage girl arrives at her sexual awakening when she learns that there's a huge subculture of people who get turned on by dressing up in animal costumes.

As the whole staff rocked in their seats around the conference table, you tried to laugh along with them. At first. But then Penny — the hot temp with bowling-ball tits —

giggled and jiggled. You weren't trying to smile and be a good sport anymore. Instead, your only aim was not to cry.

Each of your protests just made everyone laugh harder: "It's real! People who have sex in animal get ups are called furries! This is personal! You went through my desk, Tim! I don't work on my manuscript on company time! This is just a first draft! You're a real sonofabitch, Tim!"

Penny laughed so hard tears rolled down her face. Her smile threatened to split her head in two. And you so wished it would. But you don't want to hate her. You would have laughed, too. Tim really sold the funny when he read your book using his fake gay German voice. You only started to wish bladder cancer on him when he used your writerly aspirations as an example of employee sloth and distraction.

That, and when you spotted Penny kissing him in the parking lot. They were haloed in white under a light pole. You watched them from the small window by the bathroom next to your cubicle. You were working overtime again, trying to work off the stink of that Monday morning meeting. You made a big show of tearing your manuscript from Tim's hands and throwing it in the trash.

To hold the job, to hope for Penny, to pay for your shitty bachelor apartment, you gave up. You strangled your hopes and dreams for the banal. Sometimes you wish you had bladder cancer so you could stop constructing Power Point presentations for morons. If you were really sick or went out of your mind, you'd have the excuse and the escape you need.

The door to the café's kitchen creaks open. You see the tail first, long and spined, swishing back and forth as the dinosaur in a paper hat backs out carrying clean coffee pots.

You stiffen and stare. You are frozen in place.

"Good evening, sir," the dinosaur says. "Kant zleep?"

Inevitable

He walks into his living room and finds you sitting on his couch in front of his TV watching *Cake Boss*. His face works through amusing contortions. She led you to believe her bastard soon-to-be ex-husband was taller, but he's no string bean. This guy is muscled, built like a bull. Lots of newly divorced guys hit the gym hard, looking to score big with their new freedom, young and on the prowl again. This guy could be a little scary to deal with, but when he sees your black leather gloves wrapped around the pistol, screwing in the silencer, he sits on the opposite couch.

You give him a moment to process. No dummy, he works it through fairly quick, though his eyes bounce from the pistol to the rain slicker, hip waders and boots folded neatly beside you. Your black Armani suit, custom-tailored with extra room under the armpits to accommodate your shoulder holsters and exquisite, blood-red tie with the gold pin throws him, too.

He starts with the usual questions, but he can't really expect you to answer many questions. You do answer the question that amuses you, though: "You left the spare key under the flower pot. It took me about twenty seconds to find it."

He looks exasperated at that, but when you lay the next one on him, he really looks scared: "Your ex-wife says hi."

He starts screaming but wisely stops short when you raise the pistol to your lips. "Sh."

You sit back and look around his apartment. No little things to dust, so he's still alone. The place is small, like all cheap, run-down apartments for newly separated guys: Not enough light, not enough space. Except for the couches, all the furniture is the second-hand particleboard shit somebody screwed together poorly. The walls are yellowed from the chain-smoking parade of freshly minted bachelors.

"You smoke?"

He shakes his head.

"Good. Shortens your life. There are so many things that we enjoy that conspire to shorten our lives. Me? I like pie. Can't get enough cherry pie. I understand you have a similar addiction to dangerous things."

He looks at you blankly. Is it the gun in your lap that drains away IQ points?

He asks you your name.

"Jesus. Like with an *H. Hay-soose*"

He looks at you for a while. "You Italian?" he asks, looking for common ground.

"Cuban." No help for him there.

"Why'd my ex-wife send you?" he asks.

"You know why. Your addiction. Cherry? Sherry? What was the other woman's name? I forget."

He starts to babble and deny it, but when you bring up the muzzle and point it at his crotch, he covers the target with his hands and simmers down. He's sweating pretty good. She'd be pleased. His wife wanted to be here to see him sweat but you don't work that way. "Your wife — "

"Ex-wife."

"Whatever. She wanted me to torture you before the execution. She wanted to watch. I said no, but I said I'd take a few pictures just to get her off my ass. You sure can pick them, man. No offense, but she's kind of a bitch."

He nods.

"I like to feel the people.... For these jobs...I like to feel you deserve it."

"I don't deserve it, Jesus."

You take your time, watching his eyes. They do not waver. He believes it. You can hear the conviction in his voice.

"Your lack of self-awareness disappoints me," you say. "A lot of guys in your situation are pretty quick to agree they made mistakes, if only to get some credibility with me when they protest that they deserve to live."

"I married that whore twice," he says. "Marriage counseling. Everything. I tried to make it work." He looks at his hands and a tear slips down his cheek.

"You married her twice? She didn't tell me that. Marrying the same woman twice.... That's like letting the mayonnaise go bad and putting it back in the fridge and hoping it gets better when you go back to make another ham sandwich."

He shrugs. "She told me we had a kid on the way. I jumped back in shark-infested waters."

You smile. He shifts in his seat. A lot of people are uncomfortable when they see you smile. It's the one long fang. That and he keeps stealing glances at the rain slicker and hip waders and boots beside you. Finally his eyes settle on the gun. It doesn't pay to let them fantasize about taking the gun away. You train the pistol at his head while you reach inside your suit pocket. You take out the cloth wrap and open it on the coffee table one-handed. You reveal the three syringes.

"What's your plan?" he asks.

"That," you say, "depends very much on you. Sit back. Relax. Smell the crappy air and the moldy carpet as you breathe deeply. I'll tell you a bedtime story I heard the other day."

He sits back, but his gaze is on the syringes. His jaws flex as his teeth grind. If he knew about the taser in your coat pocket, the nine in your other shoulder holster, the back-up .38 in your ankle holster, the sap in the small of your back or the knife in your sock, he might give himself a stroke.

So you tell him the story. It's true and it happened in California not long ago. It's the sort of thing that makes you wonder how people find each other. Nobody pictures things going this badly when they're dressing up to march down the aisle on their wedding day.

You wait, watch his eyes, make sure he's listening instead of just looking at the pistol. He is.

"True story: this couple out in California were fighting a lot, but not quite so much that he sees what's coming. Guy comes home and she's cooked him a nice meal, his favorite. You know this guy's thinking, well, about time this bitch comes around to my way of thinking. But this woman? An artist. You know what she did?"

"She poison him?" he says.

"Good guess, but no. She drugged him. He fell asleep. When he wakes up, he's chained to a cot in the kitchen. You know what happens next?"

He doesn't answer, but his face is so pale, he sees where this is going.

"She waits till he's wide awake," you say. "You imagine that? She's so patient, she waits so he can fully appreciate his predicament. Worst thing in the world is knowing something bad is going to happen and there is absolutely nothing you can do."

"I can imagine," he says.

"Yeah. So, this woman? This woman who pledged eternal love, who'd made love to this asshole God knows how many times? She cuts off his prick. That's cold. See, I don't know you at all, but this was the man she'd slept beside. You and me, we've got nothing. But they made promises before God, you know?"

He nods.

"So she cuts off her husband's prick. There's a lot of blood with a wound like that, but she doesn't panic. A lot of people would. They change their minds half way through and botch the whole job, running out into the street, screaming and whatnot. I've seen guys piss themselves or start laughing hysterically right in the middle of a job. Not this woman. She's that pissed. All she's got left is rage."

"Not everybody's cool like you, huh?"

That surprises you. The dude might be a little okay. You give him a nod and a smile. "No. Not everyone is cool like me."

Your smile freezes him up again.

"Anyway, you know what she does with her beloved husband's prick after she cuts it off with a paring knife? She makes sure he's watching, taking it all in, and she runs it through the garbage disposal in the kitchen sink. Imagine the sound of that. Guy probably used that garbage disposal plenty of times, never thinking that one day...you know? It's the sort of thing that everybody thinks happens to other people. Nobody pulls their socks on in the morning picturing horror. The story makes you wonder what keeps people together, hating each other that much. To do that, you gotta hate somebody past hate. Regular hate? You just leave and start a new life. But this? Imagine hating somebody so much you stay!"

"Why are you telling me this?"

"I'm telling you this because when you heard that story, your dick shrunk like a turtle zipping into its shell. Your balls are trying to crawl back up into your body and hide behind your heart. Look at you. You're shiny with sweat."

"Yes."

"I'm telling you this because where other people see horror, I see inspiration. People...what they're capable of...it's amazing. Everybody starts out, just like you, standing in front of a priest, even spouting gooey vows they wrote themselves, maybe. Everything's candles and first Corinthians. People look at each other and go, 'Us? Getting married? Awesome idea.' But around fifty percent don't make it. And some of those end up where you're sitting now."

You gesture with the pistol. "You're born, you got a ticket to the human zoo every day."

"Uh-huh."

"I can see I'm boring you, so we can hurry this along. Let's talk more about you."

His eyes go huge.

You smile again and watch the shiver rock him. "They say that if you want to keep people interested, talk about everybody's favorite topic: themselves."

He nods, still thinking that maybe there's a way out of this, like his own living room isn't a slaughterhouse.

"Your ex...soon-to-be ex. She tells me you're a bad guy. She says you want more money than is reasonable. We sat down, did some math. Turns out it's cheaper for her to hire somebody like me than to keep on getting bled by you and your lawyer."

"Somebody like you," he says.

"Common problem," you say. "You've been dragging out your divorce for...how long?"

"Five years."

"Five years is too long, man."

"It's a lot of money," he says.

"Too much."

"How much is too much?" he asks.

"Nobody knows, but you know it's too much when I show up in your living room."

"What's your plan?"

"I didn't dress up for nothing, pal. How this happens is up to you."

"What if I offer you money instead? How about you kill her?"

"Not an original idea. It might be a great idea, but you don't have any money. But suppose I get greedy and get caught up in your psychodrama? I go back and she ups her offer. I'll end up feeling like a pinball bouncing back and forth between you two. Give you guys enough time, somebody will panic and call the cops, which complicates things for me. Besides, I already took the job from your wife. It wouldn't be right."

"Not right? Not right!"

You tap the gun to remind him who's running the show. "Keep your voice down. See the silencer? Funny it's called a silencer. If you think about it for longer than a second, the whole pistol is a silencer, isn't it?"

He's breathing hard. He swallows and nods.

"Nodding is good," you say. "To business."

You point at the syringes. "These are full of potassium. Sounds like I'm offering you a vitamin shot, doesn't it?"

"I'm guessing not."

"You guess right." You pick up a syringe and hold it up to the light. "Potassium will stop your heart. It's untraceable. The human body releases potassium after death. Even if they look for it, there's no set range for how much should be in the body after death. This is the perfect murder and it's not the worst way to go."

"Jesus!"

"No," you say. "Jesus, like with an *H. Hay-soose.*"

"What's my other choice?"

"Well, that's the thing. You, middle-aged guy, going through a stressful divorce that's taking forever. You have a heart attack on the couch watching...uh, there's a *Planet of the Apes* marathon on the movie channel tonight. Everybody will be surprised, but still not shocked. You die from the potassium injection. Boom. You're another one of those statistics the news is always talking about."

"Please. Another choice?"

"I'm getting to that. See, your choice will demonstrate whether you think it's better to be a brave guy or a smart guy."

"The potassium? Is that the brave choice?" he asks.

He's still hopeful. That's so cute. "No, pal. The potassium is the smart choice. The useless gesture" — you look to the pistol in your hand — "messy. Go with the gun and it's a brave gesture. It will cause quite a flap and your ex? The police will watch her for a long time. They'll ask a lot more questions than if you go quietly into that good night. A violent death will cause more trouble for all concerned, especially me. Go with the violent death and I'll have to wear my raincoat and all that."

"Fucking sadist."

"I'm not a sadist," you say. "I'm a capitalist."

He sneers at you for the first time. He's finally understanding how little he has to lose so he's thinking about giving you backtalk.

You take a deep breath and lay it out. "Choose the potassium injection, you die clean. If you don't choose the syringe, there are nine shots in this pistol's clip. The first two shots will go into your ankles. The next two? Your kneecaps. While you writhe around on the floor, I'll be putting on my raincoat and hip waders."

"That's the brave choice?"

"Brave and stupid. You're just as dead either way. That's guaranteed. Non-negotiable. If you believe in the macho bullshit of empty gestures? Die by ugly, bloody violence. You'll take a long time to die. I won't make the pain stop until the ninth bullet. You make too much noise while you're at it? I'll slip my knife between your ribs. One lung will collapse, you'll try to scream but all you'll do is bubble blood and wheeze."

His mouth hangs open.

You shrug. "Your tax dollars at work. Guys like me, we have special skill sets that don't translate so well to civilian life." You wait and watch his wheel turn and grind away on his choices.

Then, for the second time, he surprises you:

"The smart choice or the brave choice," he asks. "Which one will cost my bitch ex-wife more fucking money?"

No one's asked that before. He is brave. You smile. The truth, of course, is that the macho bullshit way will cost her more money. The hip wader way will cost her dearly. But you do something new. Without thinking about it long, you do the guy a favor and you lie. Call it charity or call it efficiency, but you'll let him die clean.

A moment later you're standing behind him. He sits on the couch, body rigid. You give him some time. If you rush it, neither of you can savor it. This is just a job, but that doesn't mean it shouldn't be done well, solemn and dignified. You are a capitalist in a fine black suit, just like a funeral director. It's nasty, but there's no need to be a dick about it.

You tell him the injection will be "just like going to sleep." This is the equivalent of a doctor saying, "Sorry. You're going to feel a little pinch." It will be more like an elephant sitting on his chest. He'll think a giant with ice-cold vice-like fingers is squeezing his heart. It will be painful, but not nine millimeter painful.

He takes another deep breath and you see his shoulders relax a little. He's not bracing for a useless fight anymore. He has accepted the inevitable. His seat on the couch may as well be a seat on a doomed passenger airliner, engines dead, mountains looming. There's absolutely nothing he can do or say to stop Fate's fall.

Good. He's ready. You place the tip of the syringe under his collarbone. Just as you're about to depress the plunger, you say, "Goodnight, Rory."

Then, for the third time, he surprises you:

"Who the fuck is Rory?"

You fumble for the sap tucked in your belt at the small of your back. "Uh...is this Melanie Drive or Melanie Crescent?"

The First Time

On the lips of sense and memory is a summer girl's kiss. Short, splashy dresses and long tan legs, she was the angel who blessed the last good July and your final free August.

Ellen came before work and worry, taxes and striving. Summer girl lived in the last gasp of autonomy and the first breath of sex. Hers was the first kiss that really meant it. You even thought the first kiss you shared might be your last first kiss. It was that good.

Women can't wear their hair long like that, but summer girls can rock that tousled cloud. Ellen was casual about her hair, a carelessness that ran so deep, she was oblivious to her power. She lived on Elm or Sycamore or Oak — one of the tree streets, high up in the hills. Her parents were absent even when they were home. Empty houses and inattention and misplaced trust meant delicious possibilities. She liked it rough, which was good, because you were too young to know how to be gentle.

Ellen said you weren't dating. You were "going with" her. (She wasn't going with you, which should have been a warning of future tears.) But you thought that if "going with" went well, you could graduate to a real relationship.

You wanted to jump straight on the boyfriend/girlfriend bandwagon, but she teased you, dragging out the wait. Ellen toyed with you, but not in a mean way. In a summer way. You anticipated every kiss and every naked moment. It was all special because it was all new.

You and Ellen were special in the way that only young people can be: certain about everything and hopeful. All that potential, all that road ahead, made you charming instead of smug and intolerable.

Time was so malleable that summer. Time stretched out and got lazy in those two hot months. You were supposed to look for work but you didn't look very far or very hard. There are only so many summers. You and Ellen knew what your parents had forgotten: the power of the pull. Poet's call them heartstrings because you can literally feel the pull when you are young.

You smelled sweet grass and sweat walked down your spine as you mowed a few neighbors' lawns, an hour or two here and there stolen from Ellen. That was all you were prepared to sacrifice. A cool shower and then quick, back to Ellen with just enough money for a movie and a box of popcorn. After, her lips tasted of butter and salt.

The Powers That Be were a sexually repressive regime. You studied 1984 in high school that spring and lived it in the summer of 1984. Your parents worried about your sex crimes, AIDS and pregnancy. They managed to hold you back from the best sex crimes of your life, but just for a little while.

The first touch was a brush of your elbow against the side of Ellen's left breast. She knew it wasn't accidental. She smiled was all, and her awkwardness reassured you, emboldened you.

The first kiss: hands in each other's hair, light frictions lighting each other's skin on fire. First some resistance, then the weight of one breast — through her dress — in your palm.

A perilous spaghetti strap hung from one naked shoulder.

Thin fabric under your fingers, her nipple pressing out.

Kisses deepened.

Unspoken needs grew to a mutual throbbing ache.

Ellen went pink, her cheeks flushed hot, her breath shortened as you trembled. You clutched at each other, holding tight, knowing where this was going. The landscape was unfamiliar, but there was no stopping that train. Time sped up again when you were alone with the summer girl. You didn't know how little time you had. Your parents might come home. You stole furtive moments. You unbuttoned her with fumbling fingers and you were too clumsy with her bra to kid her that you'd done this before.

Unsure of the way and afraid of falling, you made many forays up the mountain before you found the path to the peak. You drank in the view, blissful at the delivery of an unspoken promise that had finally arrived.

You thought you had more time. Forever stretched out in front of you, but you had no more time than anyone else. You were impatient to push forward and solve the puzzle of what you would become. You should have slowed more to savor summer moments. They only happen for the first time once: Her breath on your neck. Her tongue in your ear. Warm, sweet caresses built thirst and hunger and overpowering need.

You saw each other and you did not. Clutching in darkness, your burning night eyes saw only haloes. You spoke shining, innocent lies, but you didn't know they were lies then. They were true for a summer and the days were long and the nights were too short.

You were helpless. Her lip gloss tasted like cherries. Her long legs wrapped around you. Her lips wrapped around you. Her eyes held your loving gaze. Each time she reapplied her lip gloss, she ran her tongue across her bright white teeth.

It wasn't love, but it made you high. She was as addictive as cocaine and twice as good for you.

The War Plan

Siddown. I'll tell you a story I should have told you already. Your mom doesn't think you're ready, but the truth will set you free or set you on fire. Either way, it's the truth.

My dad, your grandfather, moved us to Wisconsin from Idaho late in the summer of 1972. We lived on Grazelle Street first. Shitty little apartment building, but years later, it was the first building I bought.

Dad moved us from a farm to this little town where he could get more carpentry work. The town's no bigger now than it was then, but I felt like a hick moving to the big city. Back in Idaho, there had been a tiny drugstore in a village ten miles away with a wire rack stocked with out-of-date bestsellers and dusty romance novels. Here we had a bookstore and a library, too, of course, so this was a big move up. I was only fifteen and until then I'd just been home schooled on the farm. Naturally, I was pretty nervous about going to a real school and meeting new kids.

Anyway, I'd only been in town for a couple of weeks before school started. I'd unpacked a little, read some comic books and rode around on my bike, but I didn't know anybody. Lots of families were away at the lake or busy with summer jobs and church camps, so by the time Labor Day came around, I was jumping out of my skin, ready to start school. It must have been the Saturday of that long weekend that I convinced my mother that I needed new duds.

Duds. You know...clothes. Okay? Yeah.

So we went down to the JC Penny's and I got her to buy me a white denim outfit, top and bottom. I remember what I really wanted was a black leather jacket but it was expensive and Mom worried that it would make me look like a hood, so that was out.

Tuesday morning rolls around and I'm looking really spiffy and cool in my white denim jacket and bell-bottoms. I'm in white except for a paisley shirt.

Sh. I'm talking.

I'm anxious to get to school so I get up early. I got my Hilroy scribblers and a brand new compass set and slide rule — No. Not that kind of compass. This was school, not the boy scouts. A slide rule? It's...never mind. Doesn't matter.

My point is, I'm ready and itching to get to school and start my new life and make friends and finally meet some new girls. I'd fooled around with some girls from church in the tall grass a few times, but our place in Idaho hadn't offered a target-rich environment, if you know what I mean. I mean, in the parlance of the day, there weren't a lot of foxes.

No.

Pretty girls is what I meant.

Are you telling the story or am I telling the story? What do you mean you don't want to hear about that? This is biography and history and life lessons, man. Don't be a prude.

Okay. Okay, good.

Where was I? Oh yeah, so I'm standing on the front step of our apartment building. I couldn't sit on the old crumbly cement steps in white pants so I stood waiting for the clock to catch up with me. Can't be the new kid in school on the first day with dirty white pants. You can get branded for life with a bad first impression. I wasn't going to risk my chances of being a big wheel on the first day by getting saddled with a nickname like "Diapers" or "Shitpants."

What's funny?

Yeah, yeah, you're hilarious.

I'm standing on the front step and what I didn't know was that old Mr. White was up on the second floor cleaning out an apartment. You don't remember Mr. White. He was before your time. He was a paradox. His last name was White but he was black. He called himself the building manager but he was really the janitor. I'm a building manager.

My mom called Mr. White "The Super." I found out later that your grandmother and old Mr. White had a thing. Well...he had a thing. I heard my parents fighting one night and your grandmother said that Mr. White's thing was like a baby's arm.

Oh, get over it. Grandma's dead. This is family history and history should be remembered. Funny, I always thought of him as old Mr. White, but he was probably not much older than I am now. But this was only 1972. Last century to you, but yesterday to me. You never know which are the best days of your life at the time.

Yeah, yeah. Can I get on with my story? You have some time pressure here, you know.

Front step. Right.

Mr. White. He was sweeping the floors upstairs and he's got a dust pan full of dirt. Without even looking, he dumps it out the open window right on my head! My brand new white outfit

191

is soiled. Totally ruins the look. Of course I start yelling, trying to get dirt out of my feathered hair and brushing myself off.

Mr. White pokes his head out the window and says, "What you standin' down there for?"

Just like that. Then he shuts the window. Sounds cold, but he wasn't really a bad guy. Just cranky. I ended up hiring Mr. White to clean my buildings a few years later. That worked for a while, until I had my dad do some carpentry at the apartment on St. James Street. Their paths crossed and they got into it.

Dad never said what they argued about, but it had to be about your grandmother, my mother. Your grandpa shot Mr. White in the hand with a nail gun. Said it was an accident, but we all knew the score. Mr. White was cool about it. I paid the hospital bill and we called it square, so your grandmother's pussy musta been some sweet, may she rest in peace.

Hey, now. You're being a prude. Sad thing, not having a sense of humor about life. All I'm saying is, these days? Anything untoward happens and somebody gets sued. Back then, men were men.

Where was I? No. No, you don't have to go. There's still time and you need to hear this before you go.

Okay...so I run back into the apartment and my jacket's a mess. A bunch of our stuff is still in boxes from the move. The Grazelle Street apartment was really tiny so we didn't even have room to open up all the boxes. Back in Idaho we had a big farmhouse. When we moved here...well, the point is, I didn't know where I could find another jacket quick.

It's getting closer to the school bell and now I'm sure I'll be late and I'm running in circles, almost in tears. Then Mom, your grandmother, pulls one of my father's jackets out of a box. It's the dorkiest orange jacket you ever saw, full of pockets and the big orange hood is pointy like a dunce cap. It had a big X in the front and back in wide yellow reflective tape. Dad wore it when he used to do roadwork for the county back in Idaho.

I don't want to wear this abomination, of course, and I'm still choking back tears. Mom tells me she'll wash my beautiful white denim jacket and I'll look cool tomorrow but, of course, she doesn't understand that tomorrow's too late. I'd go without, but it looks like rain.

Mom says "So go without a jacket and just take an umbrella."

An umbrella, she says, like we're British. That shit can fly now. I even see kids with their little brollies these days, but back then, an umbrella was something that would get you beaten up. Me? With an umbrella? Maybe by then she was so frustrated with my carrying on that she wanted to get me beaten up, come to think of it.

So I'm looking at this bright orange and yellow jacket and weighing my choices. I don't want to show up for my first day of school looking like a drowned rat in a paisley shirt with my nipples sticking out, you know? I almost asked to stay in and get home schooled for another year, I felt so bad. The only thing holding me back from chucking it all is the thought of all those townie girls I haven't visited in the tall grass yet.

I head out the door to go to school. Next thing, this little black kid falls into step beside me, looking me up and down. He sees the criss-cross of the yellow reflective tape and says, "Mr. X."

I look over and at first I thought he was a little kid but he's got more facial hair than I do. I tell him my name and he says to call him Dwayne. Turns out he's my age, but no bigger than a big crap.

Dwayne asks me if I'm the new kid on Grazelle Street but he already knows that. He'd seen me bombing around on my bike.

I'm kind of nervous, so I ask him if he knows old Mr. White. Dwayne frowns real mean and says, "Just 'cuz a brother's black doesn't mean we all know each other, man."

I'm from Idaho so I'm too quick to say sorry and he cracks up. "How many negroes you think this town has, man? Everybody knows everybody." Mr. White was his uncle. "This town is small!" he says, and he's damn sure right about that.

"Bigger than where I'm from," I tell him. Where I come from, Dwayne's a city boy. That made him laugh hard because he'd once been to Philadelphia.

I ask him about school and Dwayne gets real quiet and says it's not all bad, which tells you right there your bung hole should tighten and start worrying. Dwayne says a few of the teachers aren't indecent but his vibe is edgy.

"That's the pro. What's the con?"

"Some of the boys get kind of crazy sometimes."

"Crazy how?"

"Swirlies galore."

I'd been home schooled until I was fifteen by my mom and that never came up so I say, "What's a swirly?"

Dwayne looks at me like he just realized he is in the presence of the King of the Hicks and maybe he should curtsy or something. And he says, "Man, those crazy boys are going to drown you and flush you out to sea. I get a lot of shit because I'm small. Except for a couple of my little girl cousins in elementary, I'm the only person of the cool persuasion in school. But you? Mr. X, you might just spell me off in getting turned upside down to get dunked in the toilet."

So now I'm scared. "Shitting kittens," we used to say. Do you still say that? No? Too bad. It's a nice turn of phrase. Use it and maybe it'll come back.

Getting my head dunked in a toilet sounded like the sort of thing I should fight off. I'd been spanked plenty with a wooden spoon — we did that back then. Now you'd call it assault, but back then we called it parenting. Anyway, I'd never been in a real fistfight in my life, not even in church.

Dwayne tells me it's not a good idea to fight, though. "In my experience, that just makes it worse. I have a nice smile. I want to keep all my teeth."

"What about telling teachers?"

"Short-term solution. They'll be waiting off school property for you then. If you're a tattle and a pussy about it, things get worse."

By then we're almost to school and Dwayne has almost convinced me I'm better off running home to mama. But I tell him, "In Idaho, you're supposed to stand up to bullies."

"There's bullies and then there's bullies," Dwayne says. "Regular bullies, maybe that works. But I'm talking about boys who will one day soon be living in prison. My only solace is that one day they'll be looking out a window and I'll still be able to go outside any time I want to. They'll be thinking about how they have to deal with an ass rape in the shower and how the little guy they used to pick on is out chasing down their old girlfriends."

I tell him that sounds like a long wait and it doesn't make swirlies right.

"Dude," he says. "If an adult went after another adult like that? They don't call that bullying. They call that assault and then they call the fucking cops. We're just kids so we gotta take it and wait."

We get to school and I stick with Dwayne like glue. I've finally moved to a town and I like the idea of having a black friend. Every white guy I know likes the idea of having a black friend. Makes us feel like we're better people, though if you think about that too long, the reasoning gets murky. It wasn't all that, though. Dwayne is the only kid I know at that point, yeah, but I remember I liked that he used the word "solace." I'd never heard it spoken aloud. I thought it was cool that somebody talked like that instead of just keeping some words for books.

Also, let's face it: I needed a guide who knew the landscape. The other kids were looking at me in my bright orange dork jacket like I was some kind of freak.

In my first class, I'm the only new face. The teacher asked my name and I got through that okay, but apparently that effort kind of expended my resources. I'm used to being in a classroom that's one-on-one. Then the teacher asks what my father does. That's a weird question no one would ask now, I s'pose, but then it was reasonable, even polite. Anyway, I look around and it feels like I'm the center of the universe. I feel like I'm sitting on the toilet naked and everybody's watching with judging eyes. It's so bad, I just shrug and say, "Nothing much."

I meant no disrespect. It's just that when I stood up to speak, my brain musta fell out my ass. Your grandfather was a great carpenter and is still close to Jesus in that department. It's just that I got all balled up over details. He worked all over the place for lots of people, day to day, week to week. I should have just said construction or carpentry, but I was tongue-tied.

I'd never talked in front of that many people in my life, not even in church. Thirty pairs of eyes were looking my way and half of them were girls and maybe a third of the half were pretty cute. And I don't have a locker yet so I'm standing there in my father's huge orange roadwork jacket. I may as well have taken a bath with a skunk and added an extra dose of girl repellant.

So, anyway, when I tell the class my father does "nothing much", this big dude at the back of the room says, "How does he know when he's done then?"

That gets a huge laugh, bigger than I thought was strictly necessary. See, the big dude was a kid named Jamie Sutton. He was a boy but due to weightlifting and helpful genes, he looked like a man. His father was a lawyer and his family also owned the town's hardware store, so they weren't just what passed for rich in rural Wisconsin. They were practically the town's royalty. Jaime Sutton was their prince.

Jaime was always surrounded by his pack, too — three or four hangers on who laughed at anything their prince said. They played hockey with him and he bought the pizzas after every practice. Every summer, he let them swim in his pool up behind the big Sutton house on Beech Street. It's still there, but it's broken up into old people apartments now.

Anyway, the teacher keeps asking me questions so I can't sit down and I'm praying for a happy asteroid strike. The longer I stand there, the farther my brain crawls away from me. She asks me what I do with my free time. I shrug again because all I can think is Don't say jerk off. Don't say jerk off. Don't say jerk off. I can't say that, so all I got is a shrug.

Oh, sit still! I'm just telling you what's real. Sh!

That boy, Jaime, chimes in. "Judging by his jacket, I'd say he's hunting wabbits! Dangewous wabbits!"

That sets the girls to tittering and I know I'll never get laid now.

I was thinking this was my first day of real school and my last.

The teacher? Um. That was Mrs. Celeste. No, she was actually pretty good once I got to know her. She wasn't out to torture me. I think she was genuinely curious and prolly trying

197

to help the new kid get oriented. Or maybe she was just trying to figure out how much of a lunkhead pain in the ass I might turn out to be. She probably never met a student who had only been homeschooled and needed to figure out how far behind I was. Actually, I was ahead, but homeschooling was a weirder, hippie kind of thing back then. She probably expected I was from some hippie commune or religious cult.

Mrs. Celeste asked me one last question, maybe desperate to get a single cogent answer out of me that wasn't a shrug. By then, she might have decided I was slightly retarded, and I guess I was, socially. She asks me something you ask a little kid to gage how stupid they are. She asked me what street I lived on.

Finally I have a clear answer pop in my head so I say, too loud now, "Grazelle Street!"

"Where he hunts wabbits and the wild grazelles!" Jaime pipes up. Even Dwayne laughs at that, but I don't see the humor at all. I don't even want to go home anymore. Just kill me. I'd rather die than stay in real school. Though if I could watch all these townies trapped in a fire as the school burns to the ground before I die...for me? In that moment, that would have been optimum.

Hey. Siddown and finish your juice. I-I-I'm getting there.

My humiliation is complete. Or so I thought. When I sit in my desk, Dwayne hands me a note. It's not signed, but I know who it's from. It's not a love note. All it says is: Mr. X. Meet me in the boy's bathroom at recess. We're hunting wabbits!"

Before I know it, the clock swirls around and Dwayne's in my ear telling me not to go. He tells me he's been holding his pee since elementary school. Jaime and his pals are so bad ass, Dwayne can't pee anywhere but at home anymore.

I've got no real world experience, so I've still got some ideas of right and wrong. And it pisses me off that my best and only friend Dwayne — a guy I'd known for a little over an hour and spoken to for maybe fifteen minutes? He can't go to the bathroom unharassed. It pisses me off enough that it's guaran-damn-teed I'll go face off with the school bullies. I think I can do something about it, though I don't know what. I just think somebody should take a stand and say something.

Recess comes and I'm walking to my doom and Dwayne walks with me, telling me what a stupid move this is. "Let them call you pussy. They want me, man? They have to come out into the hall to get me. You go into that bathroom, you're asking for a dunking. They won't give you a courtesy flush first, either, if you get my meaning."

But Dwayne sticks with me. I thought it was because he was so cool, an instant friend. Much later he admitted that he thought I'd turn out to be some kind of crazy fighter who could give Jaime and all his friends black eyes. He assumed I knew what I was doing because I was heading straight at Jaime with such a head of steam.

"You couldn't talk worth shit, but the way you went down there, I thought maybe you were secretly some kind of Bruce Lee punching and kicking sort of guy."

The truth is, I thought I had to go. I thought it was the manly thing to do and being manly was a big thing. Worst thing you could do would be to do nothing if some moron called you a chicken or a pussy. That's what a manly man is, I guess: somebody too stupid to think through all his options. It's pretty dumb to pay attention to every moron's opinion.

We get into the boys' washroom and Dwayne's still dreaming I'm going to kick everybody's ass, as if life is a kung fu movie. Jaime and his buddies are already in there smoking cigarettes and they are smoking up a storm. Clouds of white smoke hang in the air. Clouds!

As soon as I walk in, Jaime yells "Wabbit!", grabs me by my jacket, whirls me around and pushes me up against the back wall. Two guys step in front of Dwayne, as if he can do anything. But Dwayne tilts his head way up to look at these guys and says, "You fellas have a good summer? I've been hanging out with my friend, Mr. X. He's got a black belt in karate. You should see him break boards and shit. He doesn't just break 'em. He shreds 'em. Man, fighting him would be like putting your face through a cheese grater and a buzz saw combined."

They all look me up and down. Lying to get out of a problem really never occurred to me. I'd spent way too much time sitting in the parlor with my mother, books on our knees.

Jaime stiffens up and puts his chin out even farther. "That right, Idaho? You learn that chopsocky, Jap-slapping bullshit between the potatoes?"

"Nope," I say. "Dwayne's just joking."

"That's too bad for you, fuckface," Jaime says.

It all makes sense in retrospect. When a guy comes on too aggressive and trying to be the alpha wolf...you know...kind of too hetero? Compensating. He's either terrified all the time and trying to look brave or, as in Jamie's case, huge gaylord, as it turned out.

What? That's what we called it, in my day. Yeah. I guess those days are over.

Anyway, Jaime looks at me like he just scraped me off the bottom of his sneakers, sucks on his cigarette and blows a cloud of smoke in my face. All his hyenas started laughing when I start coughing.

When I see Dwayne inching toward the door, I finally figure out that doing the manly thing is really me doing the idiot thing. I'd read too many comic books where the underdog prevails. I really believed that all a victim had to do was rise up and the bully would back down. I'd walked into that bathroom without a plan, without a thought in my head. I wasn't going to beat up Jaime or be his friend and no way was there going to be some miracle where they'd suddenly get enlightened and fall all over themselves apologizing for being assholes.

The only person who was getting any enlightenment here was me, and the news was not good.

I back up until my butt hits the radiator and all I can do is wait for bad things to happen to me because once it's done, the violence will be over and the humiliation can really set in deep in the bones.

I look in Jaime's eyes, which is a direct challenge to a wolf. It makes them need to attack you. Never mind that his pack is just a bunch of empty-headed assholes and the world he's dominating is a junior high school class and he's prince of a tiny Wisconsin town. He has to make sure everybody knows he owns it all. It's all animal. When I look in his eyes, I see nothing there. It occurs to me he doesn't even hate me, which makes him even scarier.

"When I grabbed you by your special jacket, little wabbit? Did I mess your hair? Maybe we should fix your hair, Mr. X. Do you like the wet look?"

I followed Jesus then, so I did the pacifist thing. It was all I had left to hang on to. I stood tall, stuck out my chin and stuffed my hands in the pockets of the hated orange jacket. And I waited a beat. Jaime gave me that moment because I'm sure I surprised him. He must have been waiting for me to put up my hands. He'd never met a Christian from Idaho.

I opened my eyes and Jaime must have seen something change in my expression. He pulled back his fist to punch me just as I slowly pulled a wrinkly old cigarette out of the bottom of a deep pocket. Only it wasn't a cigarette. It was a joint.

I was as surprised as anybody, but hid behind a smile. It was Dad's roadwork jacket, of course. On long, cold rainy days and nights, between carpentry jobs, your grandfather held a traffic sign for the county, stop on one side, slow on the other. I guess a little marijuana helped him through the doldrums of a long boring shift.

"Got a light?" I said, casual, as if I smoked up every day. Of course, I'd never held a jay in my life. I had no clue my father was, in any way, cool. He was a working man who wore plaid flannel every day. Cool and your grandfather? My dad? Impossible. I don't think I'd ever really thought of him as a person who had done anything besides measure, cut, hammer, sand and tell me to clean up my room.

As soon as Jaime saw the marijuana cigarette, his eyes go big as pie plates. He put his fist down and stepped back quick like I'd just pulled out a machine gun out of the air itself. The other guys step around Dwayne, closer to the door and they looked really scared. Two guys say, "Holy shit!" at once, in stereo.

It turns out that small town kids who are badasses are still only small-town badasses. They were just a bunch of fifteen-year-olds from Wisconsin, after all.

Jaime says, "Funny cigarette." But he says it seriously, because, hey, this was 1972.

I say, "Funny cigarette? What are you? Twelve? It's weed, man."

"Jesus!" Jaime says.

Dwayne's face is lighting up. "That whole Idaho potato thing? That's not all they grow in Idaho."

"You know where a fella might get some more of that?" Jaime says, suddenly really interested. "I might like to buy some."

"Sure," I say. "I'll be your candyman."

"The candyman can," Dwayne says.

Of course, I had no idea if my father had a stash somewhere. When I got home I tore through the rest of the boxes looking for more. It's not like I could ask my dad for weed to avoid getting black eyes and swirlies.

I never did find more of my dad's stash. Years later, your grandfather told me that was just a roadwork thing. One of the crew, the guy who laid down the hot tar? He handed out joints once in a while, just to deal with the stink and the tedium of the job. Dad told me he only took it to be polite and to fit in so the rest of the road crew wouldn't squeeze his nuts over it.

That one joint in the orange jacket, though? That kept me from getting beaten up in the boy's bathroom for almost a month. Jaime didn't come after me until he was sure I couldn't supply any sweetness. So...

You see the moral of the story, son?

Don't just be a manly man. Be a smart man. Consider all your options. Make friends with big, muscly guys. If all that doesn't work, bluffing will often get you through. You wouldn't think it unless you look close, but most people are just bluffing.

Now go get your school bag. First day of grade six can be a bugger. And pee before you go, because you have to hold it until you're all the way back home.

Context

"**I** invented a new game," Joe says as he cracks open a can of beer.

"Man, do you have to have a cold one in your hand at all times?" Lucy says, eyeing the six-pack on the floor at her feet.

"Do you have to be such a pain in the ass?" Joe asks and then takes a long pull of Fosters. The can is oversized, but almost looks small in his huge fist.

"If you're going to be like that, I can't talk to you," Lucy says. She digs a lighter out of a pocket and pulls a joint out from a pouch on her belt. She's still shaking her head as she lights up.

"You're polluting my air."

"Relax. You'll live longer and maybe a little contact high will mellow you out. This," — she holds up the jay — "would put you and me out of business if everybody just relaxed." It begins to rain and she looks out the window as she takes the first drag.

"I hate that smell. You know I hate that smell."

"Okay, I'll crack open the window and you'll barely know I'm here."

There's an empty silence between them and they both sigh. "Tell me about your fucking game," and she sucks in the smoke.

He can tell she's holding her breath, getting the most out of the weed. He takes another long drink that drains the can to half full. "You'll get lung cancer."

"Shut up," Lucy says, "you'll be in the next bed getting a liver transplant. It'll be the first transplant from a human to a gorilla."

Joe sighs. "I was listening to CBC Radio on Sunday afternoon...Cross Country Checkup."

"Yeah?" Lucy takes another long toke and her face starts to relax. Her head is tilted toward the window but she's not looking at the scenery. She is transfixed by the intricate patterns the water makes as it slides down the glass.

Joe is oblivious and getting louder. "So I'm listening to the host...uh...Rex Murphy."

"Yeah, so?"

"Murph talks to these really earnest schmoes from all over Canada. Some people, they get on there and they don't know Iraq from rock and roll but they all have an opinion about the war. But the thing is, Murphy sure can talk."

"He's from Newfoundland," Lucy says. "I love his accent. And he's very... aeriodite."

Joe frowns and gives her a stern look. "You say that like it has something to do with flight."

"Huh?"

"The word is erudite. You say aerio-dite. He's just erudite. You know, articulate?"

"Whatever."

"College girl."

"Ape man."

They both laugh and Lucy leans forward and turns up the radio.

"What's the news?"

"Big fire, but it's on the other side of town." She turns the volume down low and returns to staring out the window. "Go on, what's the game?"

"Well, I'm sitting there drinking port."

"Well, Jesus, I hope you were listening to bloody Rex Murphy on CBC Radio and drinking port with your little pinky stuck out."

"Fuck you."

"Sideways."

They laugh together again. Joe drains his beer and opens another one-handed in a smooth, practiced motion. "This beer is good stuff. Goes down like lemonade, but port is sweet and has more alcohol in it. It's meant for sipping and intellectual discussion."

"When's the last intellectual discussion you ever had?" Lucy says.

"It had to be before you and me got together."

Lucy gives him a lopsided smile and flips him one middle finger with an enthusiastic pumping motion. Then she takes another drag on her joint and stretches out in her chair a bit, visibly letting go.

"So what I notice is the way Rex Murphy talks. He's got this real college English professor thing going, except he's got that twangy Newf accent, too. I notice something and start taking a drink every time he says the word 'context.'"

Lucy begins to laugh. It bubbles up out of her and Joe can tell she's pretty high. He guzzles his beer quick to try to catch up with her. "I take it he says that a lot," she says.

"Yeah, I couldn't find the bathroom by the end of the show."

"You're such a fuckin drunk, I'm surprised you didn't settle for the word 'the' to tell you when to drink."

"I am not a drunk!" he says vehemently. Then, Joe softly concedes, "I did decide that when Murph used the word 'garrulous' I was entitled to drink the rest of the bottle down. When's the last time you ever heard the word garrulous? Nobody talks like that anymore, do they?"

"You'd know, old man. I don't even know what that means."

"You sure you went to university?"

"College, just like you."

"Not just like me. Couldn't be. If you went to college it had to be Clown College. It couldn't have been Beauty College."

"Nice. If I wasn't stoned and so easygoing I'd probably have to shoot you in the left nut. You need some weed, man. All that booze makes you mean."

"Pothead. How'd you get into taking poisonous smoke into your lungs, anyway?"

"I picked it up working for the Department of Common Vices, Scorned Virtues and Victimless Crimes."

"Do you prefer 'hophead'?"

"Doesn't matter. At least I don't drive drunk every day."

"Lucy, take that back," Joe says with real irritation now. "I am not a drunk. I'm too functional to be a drunk." He cracks open his third beer. "I was in two separate fights last Friday night and beat the shit out of two guys."

"Let me guess. Alcohol was involved."

"Of course, but none of us were more than half in the bag so mine is a fair assessment of the situation."

Lucy begins to giggle and can't seem to stop.

"Shut up!"

"...he explained," Lucy replies.

Joe sulks, finishes his beer, and opens yet another one. "For Christ sake, slow down, Joe. Make it last."

"Stuff is like water compared to port."

"Thanks, Professor Wino. That's the problem with your substance of choice. The alcohol content varies so much. You grow your own like I do and you've got a consistency. It's...really mellow, you know? I can put up with your bullshit all day as long as I stay this high."

"Pothead."

"I think you said that."

"You don't have any appreciation. You know what I love? Apple Jack on a cold night."

"The cereal?"

"No, dipshit. I'm talking apple juice and Jack Daniels, the pride of Lynchburg, Tennessee. And if I'm with a real lady — not you, obviously — I order her up peach schnapps. That's cheap, sweet class in a pretty bottle."

"Then if you both drink enough you can end up hitting each other over the head with the bottle. That's the real deal with booze. The T-shirts are right: Instant asshole, just add alcohol."

"Look at the size of me," says Joe. "I can handle my booze. Can you handle your weed? What's the last productive thing you ever said on weed? Once you're really high you get to talking and yakking and chattering and you think everything you say is brilliant, shit out of Einstein himself."

"If I was brilliant, how would you know? Einstein didn't learn to read until he was seven. He was too busy daydreaming. His teacher thought he was an idiot."

"Yeah?"

"After he was famous he said that the same level of thinking that causes problems can't solve those problems. He was probably thinking of his idiot teacher. Stupid people think geniuses are stupid. I don't judge you for not understanding me. It's not fair to expect a gorilla to do math. I want you to know I don't blame you."

"You really need to shut up now," Joe says. "If you're going to be high, be the kind of high where you just stare at your hand for a couple hours, would you? I've heard you over and over. I should tape you sometime just so you could hear yourself!"

"You don't understand, Joe." She gives him a pat on the shoulder and he can see she pities him.

"You're really trying to piss me off?"

"We'd have world peace if pot stores replaced liquor stores. Maybe what I say when I'm high doesn't make any sense to you because you've got to be high to really...really get it, you see? The right kind of high."

"We will never legalize it."

"What you mean 'we', Kemosabe? Most citizens would rather it be legalized so we can deal with real problems. Think of the taxes we're losing going weedless." She burbles her little girl giggle again. "Oh, and we could start by throwing you in jail."

"What?"

"Yeah, that sounds weird to you, but it's the same thing as tossing potheads in County just because we can't deal with life being too real. This...this is too real right now."

"You are way high."

"You know it's true. The cigarette and alcohol lobby groups shut out the marijuana lobby, That's all. It's just politics."

"Yeah. The weed whackers couldn't get themselves organized. Huge surprise there."

"If this was about what's healthy, we couldn't even eat a chocolate bar and nobody could get high except the people with prescription pain killers. Pot got shut out because a bunch of lobbyists convinced the government that pot would allow black jazz musicians to get it on with white women. Look it up. The rest was about money. That's all it's ever about. Whenever a law demands we don't let ourselves be who we are, some fat cat is making a bundle. Organized crime would lose a lot of business if weed were legalized tomorrow, so who's really on the side of law and order? How many judges and lawyers are high right now thinking, gee, I wish it were a more peaceful, happier and healthier world? Mr. Law and Order, you gotta switch your drug of choice."

"I'll tell you about 'healthy.' In a minute you're going to get the munchies and we'll have to go get nachos. Every goddamn time, you and nachos, nachos, nachos!"

"That is a silly stereotype...though now that you mention it..."

"Pothead."

"You say that like it's a bad thing," Lucy said, unperturbed. "I'm Shaggy and you're Scooby, my big talking dog. My big drunk talking dog." She starts to giggle again and this time it's really uncontrollable and she goes up and down musical scales as she collapses forward in her seat, helpless to spasms of sheer glee.

"Goddammit, Lucy! I'll break your head if you don't shut the — oh fuck!" Joe doesn't even touch the brakes as their police cruiser flies off the road.

They hit a huge, unyielding oak. Dead center.

Robert Chazz Chute

Books By Robert Chazz Chute

Fiction
Self-help for Stoners
Bigger Than Jesus
Higher Than Jesus
Hollywood Jesus, Rise of the Divine Assassin
The Divine Assassin's Playbook, Omnibus Edition
Murders Among Dead Trees
This Plague of Days, Season One
This Plague of Days, Season Two
This Plague of Days, Season, Season Three
This Plague of Days, Omnibus Edition

Poetry

The Little Book of Braingasms

Non-fiction

Crack the Indie Author Code (Book One)
Write Your Book: Aspire to Inspire (Book Two)
Six Seconds

Coming Soon
Intense Violence, Bizarre Themes
As Many Rivers to a Dark Sea / A Love Letter to Kurt Vonnegut

ABOUT THE PODCASTS

The *All That Chazz* podcast and the *Cool People Podcast* are available on iTunes and Stitcher.

The Hit Man Series

Jesus Diaz came from Cuba as a child and was kidnapped on his first day in America. Complications ensued. He's been homeless and living on the streets of New Jersey. He was a Military Policeman. Then he became an enforcer for The Machine, New York's Spanish mob. After that? *The Hit Man Series* is all about Jesus trying to find a way out. With Jesus Diaz, it's always out of the frying pan and into the napalm.

Murders Among Dead Trees

If you liked *Self-help for Stoners*, you'll love *Murders Among Dead Trees*. This fiction collection, which includes award-winning short stories, will bend your brain. A gaggle of fortunetellers, crusaders, torturers and seers are out to control you. Read it for the entertainment of psychological horror. Or take it as a serious warning about how dangerous seemingly ordinary people can be. The book includes the novella, *The Dangerous Kind* and the Poeticule Bay stories.

This Plague of Days

The *Zombie Apocalypse Series* is about two groups of refugees who survive a killer plague. The Spencer family, from Kansas City, Missouri, survive the plague that's taken North America. They must risk bio-terror, marauders and the elements to get to a hoped-for haven in Poeticule Bay, Maine. A group of European refugees face down the horrors of a virus that turns the infected into raging cannibals.

This is a monster saga told across three seasons. Reminiscent of elements of *The Stand*, the trilogy traces the evolution of new species and deadly threats as humans face extinction. The only person who stands in the way of human extinction is Jaimie Spencer, a selective mute on the autistic spectrum harboring a strange fascination for Latin phrases.

Ambitious and bold, *This Plague of Days* follows a huge arc that takes the reader on a journey that is by turns harrowing, philosophical and surreal. Do not expect the average zombie story. Each season of the saga is a unique world unto itself as the story builds to an action-packed conclusion.

Grab the *TPOD* books at the link at AllThatChazz.com or find out more at ThisPlagueOfDays.com.

Readers looking for fresh updates and more information can join the mailing list at AllThatChazz.com.

Fellow writers may also enjoy: ChazzWrites.com

ABOUT THE AUTHOR

Robert Chazz Chute is a full-time writer working from a bunker control room in Other London. A former crime reporter and columnist for newspapers and magazines, Chazz has won seven awards for his writing. Please email your comments and inquiries to expartepress@gmail.com.

Printed in Great Britain
by Amazon